RENASCENT

A PHOENIX DRAGON NOVEL 01

MAX ANDREN

ANCOR PRESS

In loving memory of my Andrea.

1

I wasn't always a bad-ass soul seeker.

Through years of confinement, I'd been conditioned to accept the inevitable until my voice had been silenced by apathy. Until I no longer had the will to fight and I refused to beg. I was so dead on the inside that I eventually died in truth.

In that moment of death, I embraced freedom once again.

For fifteen years, I'd been shuffled between various private asylums and hospitals in an attempt to find a cure for the voices that whispered and sometimes screamed through my mind.

My parents had put all their faith in these various institutions, convinced they could help me. However, after my first admission, I was only allowed home a handful of times during that first year.

My parents wanted their perfect little Snow White back— the eight-year-old me, before I had that first *episode...*

I WAS eight years old and the United States was celebrating its freedom and independence from mother England. I can remember sitting on the cafeteria floor at an assembly and singing songs in celebration with my classmates and my best friend, Jenny. It's a cherished memory—a moment when I was happy and carefree.

Jenny sat next to me and played with the ends of my long black hair as it pooled on the floor around me. This would be the last moments of our friendship. If only I'd known, I would've done something different, found some way to make it special.

This would be my last day of freedom and I would never see Jenny again.

The following night my parents, Sebastian and Helena, hosted a party for the Chicago elite, something they did on a regular basis. My father was in the finance industry and my mother sat on the board of several charity organizations. They were well connected and deeply revered.

They looked so handsome together. He was tall with brown hair and grey eyes and towered over most of the guests. Tonight, he was dressed in a grey corduroy suit. My mother had on a light-blue chiffon pants suit that complemented her petite frame, blonde hair and midnight-blue eyes.

They were an older couple or at least compared to my friends parents, as they were in their midforties. I loved watching them interact with each other and their guests. They were always so attentive to each other, their love was deep and solid.

It had been just the two of them for so long. They bonded over their struggle to conceive—bringing them closer together, instead of driving them apart. The love they shared for each other was easy to see and to feel—extra senses weren't necessary.

Other couples tended to look at them with envy. I completely understood. I was blessed to be allowed into their private world.

The evening of the party I wore a tea-length powder-blue dress with a white satin sash tied at my back, white anklet socks that had a matching blue bow and black patent Mary Jane shoes. My hair was adorned with a white ribbon and left down to curl below my waist.

Typically, I was brought downstairs by the nanny at the beginning of the evening to play the piano for the guests. My parents loved to show me off. I was a bit of a protégé and their perfect little Snow White, as they liked to call me.

I had crystal blue eyes and black hair, a nod to my Scottish heritage—or so I'd been told. My parents were open about the fact that they had adopted me from Scotland. They'd always wanted a house full of children, but hadn't been able to conceive, and so they had given up hope of ever having a child to raise.

While vacationing in Scotland with their friend, Dr.

Darren Hanley, an opportunity for adoption became available. Dr. Hanley arranged everything for my parents. They were lucky that the international laws and adoption regulations from that time, were nothing like what they are today.

Money could buy a lot—including silence, no matter the era.

My mother loved to tell the story of what their first glimpse of me had been like—apparently, I had made quite the impression. I was screaming and crying as Dr. Hanley walked out of the hospital with me in his arms.

I was six months old.

He warned them that I was a very colicky baby, but he assured them that a change in my diet would fix the colic right up.

"Your cheeks and lips were chapped red from your constant crying," she would tell me, *"and your eyes were tightly closed, so I had no idea of their color. And your wild black hair was sticking straight up! But as Darren started to hand you over to me—your bright blue eyes flew right open and you practically jumped into my arms!"*

She always recounted the memory with a smile and a happy little giggle. Even as an infant, I could *feel* her emotions and I knew how much she loved me. According to Helena, once I was held securely in her arms, I immediately stopped fussing and started cooing.

When I came downstairs to play the piano, my parents and their guests were socializing in groups and drinking martinis. They fawned over me as I made my way, slowly, to the piano.

They told me what a beautiful little girl I was—touching my hair and pinching my cheeks. I loved being at the center of their adoration and of my parents' world, but I hated to be touched by so many strangers.

I could *feel* their emotions when they touched me. Sometimes, I could *hear* them too, as their thoughts floated painfully through my mind.

I tried to explain this to my parents, but they didn't understand. They believed this sensitivity was due to my creativity and aptitude for music. They felt I was being overly emotional and imaginative—precocious even.

Not once did they believe me, but in their defense, I was outside their realm of understanding and beyond the confines of their perfect little social stratosphere. I kept the ability to hear and feel people a secret.

I was different and different meant odd and odd was frowned upon.

Playing the piano had always been easy for me, but eventually it became an obsession. It was a necessary means of expression as I grew older. Music allowed me to focus on something other than the confusion of these random voices and the pain I felt from them.

The compilation that I had created specifically for tonight was playing through my mind as I made my way over to the piano. I thought the piece would make for a fun surprise for my parents and their guests. I'd blended several classical arrangements with some current hits to create something unique and quirky. I was fairly proud of the results.

A few of the guests touched me and gave me encouraging words. I tolerated it with a smile, but the onslaught of emotions was almost crippling.

Dr. Hanley had been out of the country for several years. The last time he saw me, I was a toddler. As I passed by where he stood chatting with some other guests, he placed his hand firmly on my shoulder and gave it a tight squeeze.

I took my place next to the piano and waited for my father, Sebastian, to introduce me to their guests.

"Welcome everyone!" he said, as he settled his left hand on the same spot where Dr. Hanley had inadvertently bruised my shoulder. I tried not to flinch and smiled through the discomfort. He reached out with his other hand to beckon my mother forward.

When she joined us next to the piano, he continued to say, "My wife, Helena and I, would like to introduce to you, our daughter. She will beautifully serenade your ears off and magically prompt you to empty your pockets for Helena's latest charity."

Everyone laughed, just as they always did. And I curtsied, just as I always did, but for some reason, my heart was pounding tonight.

I looked down to see if it were noticeable under my dress

and it wasn't, but it was strong enough that I placed my hand over my heart, as if to control the runaway rhythm.

All eyes were on me—waiting and staring because I made no move to sit at the piano.

I could hardly breathe through the incapacitating fear that suddenly moved through me—a fear that was not my own. I'd felt other people's emotions before, but nothing like this and never this strong or this acute!

I was lost and drowning in the intensity.

Urine ran down my legs to puddle on the snowy white carpet below me.

I could feel my parents' mortification just before they yelled at me, but I was beyond their voices—lost in a maelstrom of terror and agony.

I grabbed the sides of my head with my little hands and pulled at my hair. I could hear a young boy screaming for mercy. I could feel his little body writhing in pain. His mind was saturated in chaos and confusion, and so was mine.

I screamed and begged with him until my voice was so raw I could no longer speak and tears poured from my unblinking eyes. I was tethered to him, as he suffered—feeling everything that he felt as he was tortured.

Mercifully, I passed out and dropped to the wet floor below me.

2

How quickly adoration turned to disdain.

Dr. Hanley jumped right in and took responsibility for my care. He had one of the guests carry me to my room, when my parents couldn't be roused to pick me up, as they had been too shocked by my outburst to move.

That was the first time I was medicated and the very last time I was touched with compassion.

Dr. Hanley had recently returned to town to take a position as the physician administrator at a small private asylum for the affluent. I was admitted to his facility and placed in his care for observation and a battery of tests.

I submitted to every treatment, Dr. Hanley and all of the subsequent doctors, put me through—all in an effort to make my parents happy. I believed they loved me and wanted me better so that I could come home.

My parents were very passionate in the beginning and

completely involved with my treatment plans. Initially that is, but I knew the truth. I could feel exactly how they felt. They couldn't hide their true emotions from my unusual and unwanted ability.

They didn't want me to come home again—not ever!

For appearance sake, they continued to come to the asylum on a regular basis. These visits followed a similar pattern—they would admonish me for making things up and I would deny that I was.

"Stop this nonsense, and behave like the daughter we know you to be!" Sebastian would demand, his face a mask of worry.

A mask that hid his true feelings, of shame and frustration, from everyone, but me!

"We want you to come home," Helena said, looking out the window, as if she wanted to escape.

We had that in common, I wanted to escape from here too.

"Don't you miss your things? Or playing the piano?" she asked.

My nose itched with the noxious scent of her fear. It was palpable from across the room and crawled through me in sickening waves of nausea.

It was obvious they didn't really want me back. There was no place for this new, *odd me* within their perfectly coiffed, color-inside-the-lines world. They just wanted their Snow White back.

I still begged to come home, despite knowing how they felt. They believed this would be the best place for me to get the help and intervention that I needed.

The next time my parents came to the asylum, it was for an unscheduled visit. Surprised, Dr. Hanley personally escorted me to the reception area.

Despite being nauseous, sweaty, and shivering, I vowed to be strong. I would not beg to come home again.

Despite my best intentions—I did just that.

"Please...Please, may I come home?"

My voice stuttered through my sobs as I tried to explain to them that I was in pain. How my back felt raw. I even reached between my shoulder blades to show them where it hurt.

Dr. Hanley explained to my parents that the drugs were playing tricks with my mind, so they completely discounted my complaints. There was nothing to see, they reassured me, but I wasn't reassured, not in the least.

"I don't see a thing. It's completely clear, except where you've been rubbing at it just now," Helena told me, after inspecting back.

"But...but, it burns terribly, like it's raw." I told them through my tears.

"It feels like when I fell off my bike. Remember? You put that stuff on my skinned knees and I cried 'cause it hurt so bad. Remember, you blew on it until it felt better?"

I was completely shocked when they told me I could come home for a trial visit.

"Thank you," I whispered with my head lowered—afraid to look at them in case they changed their minds.

Once I was home, I tried to do as my parents asked. I tired to be what they wanted, their little Snow White, but the voices inside my mind had other ideas.

They relentlessly cried for mercy and begged for help. I couldn't control them, nor could I shut them out. The constant noise was painful and debilitating. I cried often and occasionally screamed out in my sleep, which seems to be when they were at their worst.

My parents didn't know how to handle me or my supposed voices, and gave up trying. They had me readmitted, but this time to a different asylum. Dr. Hanley would no longer be my doctor, to which I was extremely thankful. Whenever I thought of being in his care, fear would flash through me and pain would ghost over my back.

That was my final trip home. I've often wondered if my parents would have rescinded my adoption, if they could have. Would they have sent me back to Scotland for a refund on damaged goods?

They were all about appearances, so of course, that would never do. Instead, I was all but forgotten. Their circle of friends were informed that I was away at boarding school, but my parents were fooling no one, least of all their friends. They all knew the truth—I was crazy.

However, in the event that a miraculous cure happened to be found, my parents made sure that I was well educated. I had the best tutors that their money could buy. I would meet with them in-between my various therapies and tried to pay attention through all the drugs the doctors fed me.

They didn't want me to be ill-bred and backwards or unable to hold a sophisticated conversation.

Who were they kidding?

It felt as if they lived in an alternate reality and it was one that I would never inhabit. None of that would matter—I would never go home again.

I had zero control over my life. None. So, I took what control that I could and that was my voice, I refused to speak. Not one word has been spoken since my final trip home.

It was during this dark, lonely time that my secret friend came to me. She kept kept me sane over the years to come. I didn't know what her name was for the longest time. We didn't really need them, but eventually she told me her name was Mia.

I cherished the fact that she trusted me with something so precious, and yet, I felt guilty because I didn't share mine too. I just couldn't.

Eventually, my parents quit trying and quit visiting. They gave the doctors free reign to implement the treatments they felt were necessary. Whatever was needed to cure me of the voices crying for mercy and whose pain was palpable, as if it were my very own. Consequently, I'd been through hundreds of cures over the past fifteen years, yet the voices remained and the emotional pain was still just as crippling.

The asylums and hospitals, I had been admitted to, were all private institutions and as such, the staff only reported to my parents. Each new doctor and every new facility did as they pleased. They loved to remind me that I belonged to them and that I was utterly worthless.

They called me a freak.

I paid for that distinction by becoming their personal lab rat. For years they tested every new drug on me in hope of finding a cure. Some of those drugs were helpful, they kept my mind quiet and the voices distant. But, some of the other drugs, stole my control and that was when my tormentors loved to strike!

I lost days and occasionally weeks at a time, with no idea what had been done to me or by whom. I would be covered in bruises and I could feel the staff gloating and I could see their spiteful, smirking faces.

I hated being so vulnerable—unaware and unable to protest or protect myself. I hated every single one of them for abusing me.

Once the drugs finally wore off and their hold over my mind lessened, I struggled to remember the lost time. But I was rarely able to recall anything and I usually gave myself a wicked headache for my troubles.

Helplessness would wash over me and I would drown in despair.

Money and influence had bought silence, stole my freedom and eventually stole my will to live...

A NEW ADMINISTRATOR had been hired to oversee the asylum. He had spent his first few weeks reviewing every treatment plan implemented. Now he was in the process of assessing every patient individually to decide whether or not their treatment plan was the correct one.

It was my turn and one of the hateful staff brought me to the admissions room.

To occupy my mind and my trembling hands while I waited for the new administrator, I picked at the frayed hem of my thin, threadbare gown. It did nothing to keep me warm, but I hadn't been given time to change.

A countless succession of nameless and faceless white coats had come and gone through the years. I'd purposely blurred the previous administrators and doctors from my memory. I shoved them into a little box in the back of my mind. I did not want or need to revisit my time with them.

I tried not to borrow trouble thinking about all the *what if's* that would accompany this new admin.

When I heard a familiar, yet unexpected voice call out my name, I looked up and froze. Visceral fear slithered through me causing my heart to race and my limbs twitch with the need to jump up and run away.

But it was futile, I was trapped and he knew it.

"Won't you even say hello to your new administrator and doctor, my dear? How long has it been now? Hmm? At least fifteen years I'd guess. You've moved around a lot, but then so have I. The law of averages was in my favor, I knew just knew you'd be in my care once again," Dr. Hanley told me from the doorway.

My time with Dr. Hanley at that first asylum had been relatively short, but that time had weighed heavily on my psyche. So much had happened there. All the initial tests and observations had been under his direction—so the pain and the trauma from that time was associated with him.

Fair or not, I hated the man with a passion!

My dreams were plagued by incomprehensible memories from my time with Dr. Hanley. A vague sense of pain and injury that wouldn't be allowed, or so I thought. I have since been disabused of that notion—anything and everything could and would be done.

No one would stop the abuse. There were no rules and no regulations, not for me.

I REMEMBER A DARK ROOM.

The smell of incense hung heavily in the air. Dr. Hanley hovered over me as I sat motionless in a chair. He muttered to himself in a chant-like fashion in a language I didn't understand.

I tried to move away, but couldn't.

"You can't move, so stop trying!" He barked at me suddenly,

causing my eyes to widen in fear—the only movement I could make.

I felt blood run down my spine from between my small shoulders where he had been carving deep into my flesh. I wanted to scream, but couldn't. Whatever he had given me, had stolen my voice and prevented me from doing so.

Except within my mind, where I screamed for mercy.

"It's strong in you! I knew it when you were a baby."

What was he talking about?

"I just knew you'd be the ultimate sacrifice and I told Hulbetto. He needs you and quickly, the others are fading—they're always fading too quickly," he told me, though I didn't understand what he meant or the disgust in his voice.

He stopped carving to gather something behind me. The burning pain on my back intensified to the point that I wanted to pass out to escape it, but couldn't.

Why—I screamed in my mind—why would my mother and father allow this?

"I knew when I touched you on your way to the piano."

I didn't mean to hear his thoughts when he touched me—I thought to myself.

"But your outburst by the piano solidified it," he told me, before he began to carve into my flesh once again.

I didn't mean to hear that little boy either—or feel his pain!

"Just a bit more on this glyph..."

"YOU REMEMBER THE REAPING," Dr. Hanley said, anger evident in his voice.

I didn't answer because I didn't know what that had been just now—memory, hallucination, fabrication? But whatever it was, the residual terror still echoed through me.

"Your parents ruined my apprenticeship!" he said, the anger escalating in his voice, "They didn't care about you and were ashamed to call you daughter. But not that day. No, they had an attack of conscience and withdrew you from the asylum. My asylum!"

Spit sprayed from his mouth and rained upon my face. I refused to wipe it off, I wouldn't give him the satisfaction of knowing how much it bothered me.

I stared at him in mute silence. The only control I had in my world was my voice—and I refused to give it to these heinous people. I hadn't spoken aloud since my last time home when I was eight.

"Still too proud and strong I see, but you'll break this time. I'll make sure of it. The reaping will be completed and my apprenticeship to Hulbetto will be finalized," he told me, a vengeful promise evident in his voice.

"Guard!" He yelled out, "Take her to the basement and solitary confinement."

The guard yanked me off the exam table. Agonizing pain flashed through my shoulder.

As the guard pulled me down the hallway, I heard Dr. Hanley say, "Let's see how you do in sensory deprivation."

3

My heart raced and I gagged as bile rushed up the back of my throat. I knew I wouldn't survive solitary confinement this time. I couldn't say that I cared. My parents would surely be relieved that I had finally cooperated and died.

No, I decided, they wouldn't care whatsoever. They had stopped visiting me years ago, I was nothing to them.

It was surprising that I hadn't died before now. I'd shamefully begged for death on more the one occasion, though only within the confines of my mind. I wouldn't allow the cries to pass over my lips.

Through the years, my various doctors had subjected me to hundreds of ridiculous therapies—including electroconvulsive therapy, periods of starvation, cryotherapy, exorcism and so many more. I was lucky that my brain hadn't been fried by their treatments or the drugs they fed me over the years.

Hanley's regimen of sensory deprivation—no light, no food and water, and no human contact, was an all-new level of hell on earth!

He was an evil, hateful man.

It was freezing in the small room where I had been *housed* and forgotten. I think that was part of Hanley's planned torture—make me wait endlessly for him to finish this reaping he mentioned. Whatever that was. Or maybe he was waiting for this Hulbetto person to show up and join the, *let's have a torture party*.

He said he was an apprentice—but an apprentice to whom and for what purpose? He was already a doctor, what more could he want? Whatever the reason for the wait, I knew I could expect more pain in my future.

My current accommodations were in the dank asylum basement, where a thick layer of mold coated the brick walls. There were no creature comforts—only creatures.

I could hear rodents circling around me, mice or rats, I couldn't say because I was blind in the lightless cell. I imagined they were waiting for me to sleep, or to die, at this point.

The disgusting creatures had no fear of me and yet, I abhorred them! They loved to creep up on me and chew on my fingers and toes, whenever I fell asleep, which wasn't often anymore.

With the first bite, I'd wake in a flash and screaming

silently. In the beginning, I would lash out with my fists and legs, but I no longer had the energy to do that. Now, I just weakly shoo'd them away and hoped they would leave me alone—and my digits intact.

Hanley abruptly stopped all my medications and now, I had no way to protect myself from the waves of emotions pouring in unhindered. I hated the drugs, but they did muffle the noise and make it somewhat manageable so that I could concentrate on other things.

As I withdrew, I had no reference for up or down; right or wrong. I was lost and drowning in a sea of pain. I shivered and writhed, then vomited and choked, as I tried to breathe and relieve my stomach at the same time.

I laid on the sweat-soaked grey and white ticking mattress trying to suppress the need to vomit again. I managed to crawl to the opposite corner, where I vomited multiple times. I could still smell the acidic bile.

The pervasive stench of mold might be the death of me— asphyxiation by mold spores, not a pleasant thought.

Every negative emotion imaginable, filled my mind in a swirling black mass of hate, loathing, and disgust. But shame was the most painful of all the emotions. It was the one I felt the most often from my parents, especially at the end.

Hopelessness and despair eroded my my soul, and without the medications to subdue the voices of the lost, the cacophony of emotions were incapacitating.

My heart stuttered under the onslaught.

As my time in solitary confinement accumulated, I created music within my mind as a diversion from the constant pain. The compilations I orchestrated gave me something to focus on instead of the screaming voices.

When I started thinking about my music this time, golden notes sparkled in the air around me. Fascinated, I watched them dance to the weeping melody of my soul—winking in-and-out of focus.

Hallucinations or a prelude to the end?

The end I thought with acceptance, but I was more than ready. I had reached that time of *knowing* and decided to go quietly.

There was no sense in crying out against the inevitable. Who would hear me? But more importantly—who would care?

I floated buoyant on a dark sea of unrelieved nothingness —numbed with cold and sensory deprivation. The only thing that kept me anchored to this side of forever was my connection to my secret friend, Mia. Her presence pulled me through the darkness of my hell, just as I tried to help her.

After my last disastrous visit home, Mia and I had connected and became inseparable, if only in my mind.

She was always with me, like now, when I'd lost the will to live. The other voices, they would come and go, but she remained constant.

We kept the horrendous details of our daily subsistence to ourselves, or as much as we could. She wanted to protect me, just as I wanted to protect her from the truth of our harsh realities.

Occasionally, when our emotions would spill through our connection, I would sense Mia's desolation. She felt encased in pain, yet surrounded by something ancient and powerful.

We were trapped in situations that neither of us could change. We were prisoners to the machinations of those with all the power.

My parents kept me incarcerated in private institutions, ashamed of who I was. I didn't know what Mia's situation was. She never explained. I knew she suffered painfully because I heard the anguish in her whispered words.

Concentrating was becoming more difficult, but I tried to focus on Mia and the distinct, emotion-free voice of my new companion. He was such a comfort to me.

The musical quality of his brogue was soothing, unlike the voices of the lost. They caused me endless amounts of pain.

"Hold on," he would tell me. *"We'll be there soon to free you."*

No one wanted me free. I had been put here on purpose— to stop the voices, yet here he was, a new voice to add to all the others.

He saved what was left of my sanity by visiting with me in my sensory-deprivation hellhole. I was beyond questioning how he spoke to my delusional mind, at this point.

He was here. I wasn't alone and that was all that mattered.

Mia was with me too, though I barely felt her now.

I allowed myself the comfort in believing that they were both real, though I knew it was a lie. He was a figment of my deranged mind, just as Mia was.

Despite their presence and the comfort they freely offered, I decided to quietly fade away. I would retain what small measure of dignity I had left, however fleeting it may be.

I didn't realize that my eyes were open until a ribbon of blue iridescence shimmered past and captured my fixed gaze. I wanted to touch that comforting glow. I longed to hold its warmth against my freezing soul.

I reached out a trembling hand, but it vanished and I wept silently within my mind.

Again, I knew nothing but darkness,

4

Time was irrelevant when there was no benchmark to gauge it by, so I had no idea of its passage. Moments or perhaps days later, the blue iridescence was back.

It felt both sentient and masculine and a protective warmth enveloped me. The ribbon of light shimmered through the darkness, but I closed my eyes, preferring blindness to the reality of my dungeon hell.

My companion's distinct voice whispered through my mind again, feeling closer.

Had he returned to escort me on my final journey? I would have cried, if I could have.

I wouldn't be alone.

"You have been very difficult to find," he said within my mind.

"Who are you?" I asked in kind.

"My name is Cipriano."

"How do I hear you and above all the others?"

"I've lived a long time and can shield you from the other voices, diminishing their volume."

"If I begged, would you stay with me for a while? Could you keep the voices of the lost subdued so that I can fade away—in peace and quiet?"

"There will be no fading," he demanded of me, his brogue thickening when he added, *"you will fight!"*

I closed my eyes in shame at the vehemence of his emotions. I had no will to live. I had nothing left to fight for, especially now that Mia was fading away too.

"I hear all that you wish to hide. But you mustn't give up. Have faith. I'm on my way there, Pena."

Cipriano began telling me stories of his homeland. He described them so perfectly that when he projected the scenery directly into my mind, it was exactly as I had envisioned.

I knew he was a hallucination, as were the stories and the pictures he shared with me. But at the same time, they had helped to alleviate the pain caused by the sensory deprivation of my dungeon hell.

The combination of the voices of the lost, the cold, the hunger and the horrible drug withdrawal, were warping my reality, but at this point I didn't care. My heart was beating erratically and took my breath away.

"Won't you tell me your name?" He asked me at one point.

"I CAN'T. All I know...all that I feel...is pain," I said breathlessly.

AND SO BEGAN his fairytale stories of mythical dragons. The majestic and beautifully scaled creatures came to life within my delusional mind. Mia and I had always loved dragons. It was strange that my companion, Cipriano, would speak so eloquently of them too, but I didn't question it. I chose to enjoy every moment of escape, envisioning his descriptions, versus dwelling on the here-and-now.

Through him, I experienced what it was like to fly high above the snowcapped Highland mountains of Scotland. Where the crisp air flowed over his scales and under his wings.

He glided effortlessly—scaling up one side of the mountain and down to the deep glen on the other, where purple heather waved in the wake of his passage. His projections into my mind were crystal clear, as if I were watching a movie.

We flew over blue lochs that perfectly mirrored the sky above and the colorful dragons within. Cipriano surprised me by skimming the surface of Loch Ness with his dragon claws. I looked below the surface for Nessy, but I didn't see her.

Perhaps my Cipriano was the cause of such rumors and legend. When I asked him, he would neither confirm, nor deny the possibility, that he and his brothers purposely perpetuated the legend of Loch Ness.

One night, Cipriano took me to the Isle of Skye with his stories and I fell in love with the Fairy Pools. They became one of my favorite destinations to escape to within my mind. They were mystical and sensed their magic through his memories.

The Fairy Pools were a natural waterfall and collection of vivid blue and green pools, surrounded by rocks, heather, and boggy areas. At the head of the pools, looming over them like an overprotective parent, stood the serrated ridge of the Black Cuillin mountains.

I wish I could have truly visited the Fairy Pools before I died. They called to me, the whole country felt like home. But Cipriano gave me the next best thing with his visions—he gave me a taste of freedom. It helped to beat back the claustrophobic feeling of suffocation that slowly consumed me as I lay dying in my lightless dungeon grave.

He shared the love he had for his brothers and briefly, I was able to experience what it felt like to have a family bond that went bone deep. They were connected beyond mere brotherhood.

I had always longed for that feeling, that sense of family. I had it briefly as a child, but even then it felt weighted by condition. If I behaved in a certain manner, then it flowed freely and without reserve. When I was their little Snow White, all was well within my parents' world. But when I didn't conform to their reality, I felt their disappointment and their shame.

Unlike normal children, I really could feel what they felt, even though they had no idea that I could. Or rather never believed that I could.

The wonderful vignettes Cipriano shared with me about his brothers were treasured moments that I brought out to review when I was cold and alone and waiting to die. I'm sure he had no idea what he had given me—a gift beyond measure and without compare.

He had given me solace.

Through the years, I had refused to beg my tormentors for anything, and therefore denying them the satisfaction of my voice. But, I would willingly beg Cipriano for more stories, more scenery, just more of his interesting dragon life.

I shared his stories and visions with Mia. She and I had loved to make up stories about fantastical creatures and far away lands where mythical dragons flew through the night sky, as fierce warriors to the rescue.

Ours stories, or rather mine, were nothing compared to what Cipriano shared. His insight and detail went far beyond anything that I could've imagined.

Cipriano always shielded his emotions from me, which was why he was such a comfort. But occasionally, when he spoke of his brothers, I could feel his sadness and grief.

"Will you tell me about your brothers?" I asked the voice of the companion of my mind.

Perhaps, in sharing the burden of his grief, it would

decrease the pain in his soul. It was that one pivotal question that had solidified our bond.

Rationally, I knew all of this was conjured with my mind, but the connection I felt with Cipriano seemed so real. After that question, I learned all about drampires and their hate for all dragons, but especially, Cipriano and his brothers.

"I've been alive since the Crusades," he told me, shocking me with his age.

"Dragons have always been protectors and for male dragons, it's innate. Though there have been plenty of female warriors over the centuries. My father, Laurent, had met a Scottish nobleman who had come to the Middle East on his first crusade. This man had employed my father as his private guardsman."

Initially, his father had kept secret the fact that he was a dragon. But, Laurent and the nobleman had bonded, which led his father to eventually confess the truth.

"Laurent had several brothers, but they were also dragon leaders, so he decided to take his mate and return to Scotland with his nobleman where he formed his own clan."

Cipriano and his two brothers, Aiden and Jakoi, were born in Scotland and followed in their father's footsteps becoming guardians to the Scottish aristocracy. The trouble came with the neighboring clan of druids.

"We kept to ourselves, but we weren't exactly hiding either. Because of that, the neighboring druid clan caught onto our longevity and envied our immortality, so over time, we became enemies."

The druids found a way to hijack the coveted immortality from dragons by mortally wounding a full-fledged dragon. Once wounded they would steal the dragons' essence to acquire infinite immortality.

"It was the perfect method to steal and harness our immortality to fuel their own. But it's not that easy to acquire. No dragon would willingly give up their essence—their very soul to a druid. The druids became creative and devised a way to attain immortality without stealing it from a full-fledged dragon. They have a knack for finding our brethren with dragon blood."

"Once located, they capture our brethren and perform a reaping ceremony by carving dark magic glyphs into the skin of their victims with a ceremonial blade made from Damascus steel. They torture them to death and reap their adrenaline-laden and traumatic emotional energy during the process. This energy is funneled into a Damascus amulet and adorned with a bloodstone."

"That's horrible."

I couldn't comprehend that kind of evil, though I had felt it myself.

"They wear the amulet around their necks and the trapped energy they stole provides them with extended life. The effect of the reaping is short lived and must be replenished over and over. And so this is how the drampire was born."

"Why don't the brethren try to fight or escape?"

I remembered how I wasn't able to move when Dr. Hanley had me in that room and was carving into my skin.

"Damascus is a type of ancient steel and it's a known paralytic for dragons, much like kryptonite is for Superman."

It was strange to hear this centuries-old dragon talk about Superman.

"I've been to the movies, though it's been quite some time."

"I haven't either."

"It's important to keep up on current events. I am ancient, but don't want to appear as such."

He told me about Hulbetto, one of the longest living drampires. He had been around since the crusades and he had tried to kill Cipriano multiple times throughout the centuries. He was responsible for the death of one Cipriano's brothers and the cursing of another. He didn't tell those stories, but I sensed a tremendous amount of pain and grief.

For centuries, Cipriano has been searching for his brother, Aiden. I felt his determination to find him, wherever he was. If Aiden was real, that is—if any of this was real.

I wanted Cipriano and all his wonderful stories to be real, but at this point, it didn't matter.

My time was over, I could feel it...

THE BLUE IRIDESCENCE that was Cipriano, slid across my lips to offer what felt like sustenance. My heart ceased with its rapid stuttering almost instantaneously. It began to beat with a regularity that I hadn't known in a long while.

"What did you do?"

"I offered you a bit of my life force or essence—if you will. It's very diluted, as I'm not really here and only an astral projection. But when I arrive to free you from hell, I will give you a proper offering."

I didn't understand what he was trying to say and help was so foreign to me that I didn't know how to respond.

"You're just a vivid apparition of my deranged mind," I dismissed.

"You're not deranged and I'll prove it to you once I'm there. But, for now you must fight."

"You're too late," I said, as I felt my heart stutter again, *"but thank you for these precious moments of respite."*

"You will not fade!" Echoed through my mind, but I was beyond responding and took my final breath—welcoming death.

5

With that final breath I was consumed and surrounded by—nothing.

The stuttering cadence of my heart was silent. My breath ceased to rasp in and out of my lungs. Pain, my constant companion since I was eight years old, was blessedly absent —a precious gift that only took dying to obtain.

There was no white light to behold. There was nothing.

Nothing, but quiescence—at long last...

I found myself outside standing on the courtyard's vibrant green lawn with no idea of how I arrived there. I couldn't feel the prickly blades of grass beneath my feet because I was no longer corporeal—I had no body. I felt insubstantial, like a dandelion floating on the wind.

The perpetual setting sun caught my attention as it sank below the horizon and brought closure to the day and to my life. My final dusking sky was illuminated in shades of pink, orange, and blue—an exquisite light display with far too many colors to name.

The sun finished its nightly descent and I waited to make mine. Given what my parents and the staff had thought about me, I would be descending straight to hell.

Having no idea what to do next, I did nothing at all.

A flock of birds in a tight V formation made their way across the rising moon. I was mesmerized by the way they flew in unison and yet, could make such quick directional changes without flying into one another.

The flock of *birds* landed on the grass before me and still in formation. I stared at them in disbelief—dragons? I blinked my eyes, but they still didn't vanish

Five *dragons* had come to escort me straight to hell.

They were about the size of a van. They had seemed so much smaller flying through the sky.

Who knew that such magnificent creatures would be utilized to escort, the dead and their damned souls, to the other side.

I should have been afraid, but I wasn't. Between the colorful stories Cipriano had shared with and the ones Mia and I had created together, I felt deeply connected to these mythical creatures.

Mesmerized by their colorful scales, I quickly projected their images to Mia. I illustrated how the sunset had paled by comparison, but I could no longer feel her within my mind.

She was gone and painfully silent.

The dragons shimmered before me and I could feel the static electricity humming through the air. They wavered and so did my stomach—which should have been impossible considering I was dead.

Standing before me and where the dragons had been, were four men and one woman. I blinked my eyes again, but this time in confusion and then in disbelief at what I had just witnessed.

The one standing at point walked towards me.

"Where are you, Pena?" He asked with his mind and in a familiar voice.

"I am before you, as you can see," I answered in kind, then thought to ask him who he was, though I thought I already knew the answer.

"Time is diminishing, Sister. Where is your body then?"

"In the dungeon basement," I replied.

He took his hands and placed them over his heart and whispered quietly to himself. It appeared as if he were gathering something and I saw that he was. Within the cradle of his cupped hands was the same glowing blue iridescence that had visited me in my dungeon hellhole.

I looked at his face and then at his hands. I thought about how his voice had sounded in my mind and realized he was indeed my companion. He was my blue iridescence, as well as a dragon and a man.

He nodded. "Come Sister, drink of my essence and be

risen. Be Renascent," he told me formally and aloud for the sake of the others.

"I don't wish to be risen or whatever it is that you're offering. I welcome death! I'm thankful it has finally found me," I said stepping backwards, away from his proffered hands.

"I understand wanting to have your final rest and finding that peace you were denied the whole of your life. But you need to drink. For her sake, you must," he told me, as he walked forward.

"Who is she? Who must I drink for? There is only me and I do not wish to."

"Your mind seems still, but I'm there with you and I can hear her. She's very quiet, but if you focus, you will find her. The two of you are connected. You will need each other, but only you can find her," he explained.

I didn't understand his explanation at all. He spoke in circles of nonsense, but I tried to do as he asked and searched my mind. Besides, the longer I was dead—chances were, I would stay that way.

My mind was calm and quiet, but I was so used to the constant chaos and the never-ending cries of the lost, that the silence was eerie. I closed my eyes to concentrate, but I heard nothing.

I felt nothing.

I wanted to prolong the time since I had died, so I waited a bit longer before giving up the search for *her*. But then I found her quietly weeping and now that I heard her, I could feel her too. Her hopelessness nearly broke my already dead heart.

It was Mia! She was still there, though barely.

I hadn't made her up.

She was real and my relief was instantaneous. But in that moment, she reminded me of the little boy I heard all those years ago. His fear and pain—so real to me—had triggered the empathic episode that caused my parents to have me committed. I didn't want her to suffer as he had suffered.

I opened my eyes to see Cipriano's hands patiently offering me his blue iridescence. I heard *her* quietly begging to '*please, help*' and with that heart wrenching plea, I stepped forward to accept his essence.

I drank, no matter the cost or potential consequences.

Mia and I had been together for years. I would find and deliver her from whatever hell she was consigned to.

For a brief moment, I felt nothing except a profound sense of peace and wellbeing.

Then I knew nothing at all.

6

A benefit of being so cold was that my metabolism had dramatically slowed. My body had needed less oxygen to survive so there would be minimal damage from my dead time—if any at all.

After Cipriano shared his life force with me, my essence had returned to the dungeon and reentered my body. I had risen, Renascent, but had not been fully healed. I was alive, but my body remained weak from malnutrition and malicious neglect. Unfortunately, my mind returned to its usual state of chaos.

Oddly comforting, though loud and painful.

I was in the asylum basement when Cipriano materialized before me. His beautiful blue iridescence glowing in his hand so that we could see in the pitch-black dungeon. Three of the others materialized around me—transforming from mere shadows to men once again.

What a cool ability to have I thought inanely and shook my head at all the strange and wondrous things I'd witnessed since dying and becoming Renascent.

Cipriano bent down to gather my slight frame into his arms and carried me away from what would have been my final internment. The open sky was much preferable to my dank hell. But first, we would have to find a way past the guards and the staff.

"The others are clearing a path for us to leave this place unmolested."

Too late for that, I muttered within my mind, then blushed when I realized he probably meant leaving without anyone trying to stop us. I was thankful I hadn't projected that thought to him.

I realized he had heard my wayward thought when he said, "And they will pay for that as well!" Retribution evident in his voice.

Once we were outside, Cipriano knelt down with me still in his arms and placed me gently on the lawn in the courtyard.

"Sister, if you please, rest here a moment with Ian. We have one more thing to take care of and then you will be rid of this place for good," Cipriano said, but stayed kneeling.

I looked at him questioningly.

"If you would permit me, I would be honored to seek vengeance on your behalf," he said or asked, depending on how you wanted to classify it.

He was like a warrior of old seeking my permission to do battle.

I nodded because I didn't trust my voice to work. I couldn't say it within my own mind either. Besides, I wouldn't be able to hurt a fly at the moment, if ever.

Nodding back, he placed his fist over his heart and bowed his head for a moment before standing. He and the others transformed back to shadows then disappeared within a blink, blending with the natural shadows cast by the moon.

I looked up at Ian and asked, *"How...how do they do that?"* I stuttered through my mind, as I tried and failed miserably to formulate my thoughts into some semblance of order. I had seen so many amazing things it was hard to grasp them all.

He chuckled and said, "Quite disturbing, is it not?"

Ian nodded when I realized he had heard me with his mind, but he confirmed it by saying, "Yes, I can hear you too. We all can. You are quite loud, Pena," he finished with a smile and a wink.

"Why do you call me that?"

"We are Scottish, among other things, but in our culture Pena means sister. So you are and shall be."

These five strangers were treating me as if I had value, as if I were something more than nothing. I had no idea how to respond to this anomaly and so I didn't respond at all.

I pulled my knees to my chest and wrapped my thin arms around them. My threadbare gown hung dejectedly on my skeleton-frame and did little to protect me against the cool night air.

Warmth enveloped my shoulders and brief, hazy flashes from Ian's life fluttered through my mind, as I felt his warm jacket settle against my filthy skin. I allowed myself a moment of selfishness to enjoy the thoughtfulness of his gesture and the warmth his jacket provided.

With regret, I shrugged it off and handed it back to him, saying as I did so, *"Thank you, Ian, but I can't accept your jacket. It wouldn't be right."*

I'm too filthy, I thought to myself.

"No, Sister! You are not filthy and you will cease in thinking so!" he said, as he settled the jacket back around my shoulders.

I hadn't meant for him to hear that last part. I really needed to work on not projecting my every thought, but I was too weak and too tired to censor myself or argue about the jacket. Without Cipriano shielding me, the voices were roaring out of control and a bit louder than usual.

Luckily, I was still sitting on the grass because I was blind-sided by disorienting vignettes of death that suddenly flashed in-and-out of focus within my mind. I saw the others in their dragon-form circling Dr. Hanley and the asylum guards. They were standing within the inner courtyard where the dragons had placed them.

I couldn't direct the vision because it were coming from Cipriano I realized. The mental scene switched to panning the buildings surrounding the courtyard. I saw the many faces of the deranged pressed against the glass—silent witnesses—waiting and watching, knowing this would affect their fates as well.

The scene returned to Hanley and the guards, now bloody and covered in deep gashes. The dragons were toying with them, like the cat does the mouse. There was no sport in it for Cipriano and the others, so they cut the chase and went straight for the killing blows.

My next vision was from above. I saw what appeared to be a dragon's claw slash across the throat of one of the ten guards. A spray of blood arced outward as his body twisted and fell. Eyes widened in shock, he clutched his throat as blood bubbled out from his gasping mouth.

Each of the guards followed in a similar fashion. I witnessed to the entire death scene within the landscape of my mind. The dragons killed them all and without remorse.

Hanley was the only one left standing. He was bleeding from multiple gashes, including a bone deep laceration across his forehead that bled profusely into his right eye. I couldn't hear what he was saying, but I could *feel* his fear as he begged for his life.

I was in Cipriano's mind watching and feeling everything. He said nothing and I felt nothing from him—only from Hanley. I reached out to Cipriano to stop his killing blow. Stumbling as I stood, I made my way towards them.

"He'll not be happy that you saw that side of him," Ian stated when I looked up at him.

As weak as I was, it was slow going. Without asking, Ian picked me up and carried me, but once we were almost there, but still out of eyesight, he placed me on the grass.

I took his jacket from my shoulders and handed it back to him and said, *"Thank you, for its use, Ian."*

With my chin up and my head held high, I walked the rest of the way on my own volition. The staff and guards who had repeatedly abused me and their authority, were dead and scattered around the courtyard—dismissed. I ignored their bloody bodies and walked towards Cipriano.

The dragons were acutely focused on Hanley and so was I.

Hanley was looking between Cipriano, in his dragon-form and me, as I walked up and stood next to Cipriano's side. Without Ian's jacket, I was freezing, so I locked my knees.

I would not shiver. I would not fall over. Period!

Staring at Hanley, I refused to acknowledge my weaknesses, all courtesy of his heinous dungeon deprivation treatment.

A flash of red hazed through my mind just before I saw Cipriano's dragon claws lash out with macabre silence to rip the good doctor's heart right out of his chest. He collapsed, as if in slow motion—a puppet with its lead strings suddenly cut.

I looked around at the carnage then down at my most recent

tormentor and finally at Cipriano. On shaking legs, I turned to face him placing the death scene at my back. He looked at me briefly with his expressive grey eyes, then bowed his dragon's head—in apology, understanding, and vindication all at once.

I stood before Cipriano, his head still bowed, as he waited for what I would do. He held Hanley's beating heart within his claws, an offering of sorts, for vengeance sought and justice served.

A sensation that could not be named and a compulsion that would not be denied crept through my body, consuming me like wildfire. I reached out my hand to press two of my fingers against Hanley's beating heart. It was still warm and wet, and resonated evil from where I touched it.

Reaching out with my other hand, I placed it along Cipriano's massive jaw and gently raised his face to mine. When our somber eyes met, I nodded my head.

He closed his claws around Hanley's heart and crushed it with his talons, letting it fall to the ground below—unnoticed.

Compelled beyond reason, I simultaneously took my bloody fingers and wiped them across the glyph on my back. Until recently, I had no idea that it even existed. Hanley had carved the glyph into my back when I was eight years old.

"Stop, Sister. Do not!" I heard Cipriano yell through my mind.

He was too late. On some instinctual level, I knew I needed Hanley's Druid blood for the dark magic that it contained. I didn't want to be tied to his evil power, but this moment felt ordained.

The glyph began burning. I could feel his dark magic seeking to possess me, looking for a way to turn me from good to evil, but that would never happen. I would use his dark magic to *my* benefit, I would use *it* to find and defeat other drampires.

I would not be used. Never again!

Still not trusting my voice to work, I spoke to Cipriano with my mind and simply said, *"Thank you."*

"I'm sorry you had to witness their deaths. I should have protected you from that," he replied quietly in the same way.

"No one has protected me in a very long time and you sought justice for the wrongs perpetrated against me," I paused to point to the faces in the windows, *"and to all of them. These 'people' deserved to die for the atrocities they subjected us to. We were helpless and in their care. They abused us from their position of power. We had no recourse, so I'll not mourn for them,"* I replied with a definitive nod. *"What will happen to all the patients left inside?"*

I couldn't stand the thought that they might suffer because of me.

"They will not be made to suffer and least of all because of you. I'll send someone I trust to come and assist them. We will find proper treatment programs with true hospitals to care for them. Nothing like this one."

"Thank you," I said and collapsed where I stood.

7

The excitement of the rescue, my confinement, dying and having risen Renascent had finally proven to be too much. Luckily, Cipriano swooped me up into his dragon arms before I ever hit the damp ground.

When I awoke, a short time later, I was cradled in his human arms as he rested on the grass. I looked at him wide-eyed and slid off his lap. I was no longer comfortable with demonstrative acts of kindness. I didn't know how to process them, as they were so far outside my usual experience of psychological and physical abuse.

"I'm really not the fainting type, but thank you for catching me."

"Will you tell me your name?"

I didn't want the name my adoptive parents had given me. Names had power. My parents and the doctors had stripped all the power from that one, so I had decided to choose another one for myself.

"That's a great idea. Be Renascent—reborn—in this moment. Define yourself. Don't be defined or confined by them."

"*Sage advice,*" I told him, "*it's weird that we can talk this way, but thank you for shielding me from the other voices and their pain. I needed the break.*"

"*I cannot talk to everyone in this fashion. You are unique in that.*"

"*What are you?*" I asked, then hesitantly added, "*besides a dragon?*"

"I'm just an old warrior on a quest to find his lost brother."

I could easily believe that he was a warrior and a leader of people. He was tall and muscular and carried the mantle of responsibility with ease. He had grey eyes and longish dark hair that had a white streak running from his right temple.

"*Those stories you so generously shared with me as I lay dying, were they all true?*" I asked. They had helped me to focus on something besides the pain and my impending death.

"Yes. Just a few snapshots from my long life."

"*I loved the freedom I felt when flying over the mountains and skimming the lakes. I haven't had that sense of joy in more years than imaginable.*"

"I know, Pena. I've been searching for you for a while now."

"*One day blended with the next—add in all the drugs they fed me, it's really hard to know how much time passed. But why were you searching for me?"* I asked, looking around as I waited for his response.

I noticed there were piles of ash around the courtyard that hadn't been there before. I wondered where they'd come from. Fascinated, I watched as handfuls were lifted up and carried away on a gentle wind. I looked back to Cipriano, thinking he would have answered my question by now.

"I apologize for being rude. I promise to listen to your answer," I said, embarrassed for having been less than attentive.

"Pena, there is absolutely no reason for you to apologize. I was merely waiting to see if you would answer your own internal question about where the piles of ash had come from."

I tilted my head to look at him and thought about what he was trying to convey. I looked around the courtyard again—to *see* this time. The grass was devoid of dead bodies! I swung my gaze back to Cipriano and he succinctly explained in just two words.

Dragon fire.

I nodded, that made sense, I guess, *"But why?"*

"We can't *justifiably* rip these men apart and then leave them for normals to find."

"Normals?" I asked, interrupting.

"Normals are what we call people without any kind of magic in their soul. They can't shift to any other form and are stuck as humans. So in other words," he shrugged his shoulder and said after a pause, "normal."

"I see. So like me. I'm basically normal, except that I can hear and feel people. I don't have magic in my soul or I would have used it long ago to escape from this hell on earth."

"You are anything but normal, but we'll save that for another day. For now, let's go home."

Home, I shook my head, I didn't have a home.

"You do now."

Tears clogged my throat, but would never dare to fall. I learned that lesson the hard way over the years. Never, ever let them sense your weakness or they would capitalize on it, and painfully so.

My attention was drawn to the others as they made their way over to us. There was the lone female, Ian and the two other men that looked like they could be twins.

"They are."

I glared at Cipriano and he smiled back. First things first, I would have to learn how to keep him and the others out of my head.

"Tarrin and Tauric, along with Isabella," he told me, by way of introduction, then continued to say, "my family by choice and yours as well, should you choose us."

I didn't say anything because at this point, there was nothing to say.

"Are there any belongings that you want to collect before we leave?"

"There's nothing. I'm ready to leave whenever you are."

Nausea was rearing its ugly head again. I fought the need to dry heave the emptiness of my stomach. Cipriano must have sensed my struggles and told me we were leaving in a moment. He reached out to me with the blue iridescence of his calming essence. The shielding effect was so much stronger now that he was standing next to me and not an astral projection like before.

The nausea improved and for the first time in my life, I felt something other than pain and suffering. I didn't have a name for what I felt. At a guess, I'd call it compassion and it was coming from Cipriano and the others. I had no frame of reference for how to handle the emotion and as a result, I felt squirmy and uncomfortable on the inside.

Everyone except Ian shifted into their dragon-form. He had waited so that he could place me gently upon the back of Cipriano's dragon. I caught myself wanting to pet Cipriano and barely refrained from doing so.

His iridescent scales just begged for me to touch them. They were soft beneath my bared legs, like worn leather, not at all rough, like I thought they would be.

Once settled, Ian gave me his jacket again. I thanked him and did as he told me to, which was to hold on. Once Ian shifted, we flew away. I chose to look towards my new future, instead of back at the painful past I was leaving behind.

Flying upon Cipriano was even more exhilarating than I

could've ever imagined. I tried to link with Mia to share it with her, but she still felt weak.

Cipriano told me he chose his family and that I could do the same. Mia would be my first choice. I projected that to her and felt a ripple of acceptance and gratitude for my choice and for sharing my flight across the pale pink sky of dawn.

After my rescue from hell, Cipriano brought me to his mansion on the outskirts of Kansas City. I wouldn't appreciate the beauty of his home until much later. After I learned what it meant to be Renascent, who I was, and what I was meant to do.

8

I had so much to learn, but first and foremost I needed to get well and heal from my confinement in the dungeon. Malnutrition and neglect had taken its toll upon my body, though it had helped becoming Renascent.

After all, I was alive.

When we first arrived at the massive estate, I was too tired to appreciate its beauty—exhaustion pulled hard at me. I felt ready to fall sleep where I stood, but it had been a long time since I felt comfortable enough to let my guard down enough to sleep. I had to be on guard for the rats—both the two and four-legged variety.

The bedroom where Isabella brought me was beautifully decorated in varying shades of creamy yellow. It was like a bashful morning sunshine had been captured and painted upon the walls.

I loved it! Especially after weeks of darkness and years of

staring at putrid green walls—walls meant to calm our supposedly unstable minds. Ha, it was the most nauseating color I had ever seen and made us all look jaundiced.

I looked down at myself and cringed. I was filthy and I stank. I don't know how Cipriano and the others could stand being around me, let alone fly here with me on his back. At least while flying, I had air movement in my favor. I decided it was best not to touch anything.

While Isabella gathered things for my shower, I tired my best to clean the dirt and bloody remnants off my hands. I wiped them down the sides of my stained gown where the filth was likely to blend in.

Raising my hands for inspection, I quickly hid them behind my back when Isabella turned to ask me a question, but she had seen.

"Thank you for your thoughtfulness, Isabella." I said, hoping to draw her attention away from the embarrassment of my condition. *"I apologize for the mess I'm making. I'm so dirty,"* I confessed, through mind speak.

"Nonsense. You are not responsible for the conditions those heathens kept you in. There's no need to apologize for their reprehensible behavior. I'd like to rip their throats out again!" she said angrily, then tempered her tone, to say regretfully, "I'm more than sorry we weren't able to find you sooner. We've looked for years, you know?" she informed me.

I shook my head.

"We have, well mostly Cipriano has. He was the one that

was most able to connect with you, though we could all hear you," she finished.

Isabella walked over to turn on the shower, though I could have done so and then left so that I could bathe in peace. She didn't go far and stayed right outside the door just in case I should need her. She expressed her concern that I'd become overwhelmed by pain, nausea or weakness—or by the lost ones crying for mercy in my head.

Lord, I was a complete mess physically, mentally and emotionally.

I hadn't had a proper shower in far too long and it felt heavenly. I was still cold and stood under the spray of hot water in an attempt to alleviate the chill. It had settled deep into my bones, but it would take more than hot water to relieve that particular ache.

Multiple scrubbings with soap and hot water had cleansed my skin of what felt like years of filth. If only it were that easy to cleanse my soul. So while my soul didn't feel all shiny and new—at least I no longer felt dirty and unkempt.

Ian brought me a rich and nutritious mug of bone broth to drink. At first I was hesitant. But after he explained, it was just chicken broth that had been cooked with the bones still in the chicken to reap the nutritional benefits of the marrow, I sipped at the delicious broth knowing I needed it.

There was that word again—reap. I glanced at Cipriano who had come to see me just as I had settled into bed. As I sipped from the mug, I wondered if he would know what Hanley had been referring to.

"I do. But we will get to that later. Right now, finish your broth and then there are a few things that I would like to teach you before you go to sleep."

I wanted to chug the broth, so he'd tell what I needed to know, but I knew if I did, I'd vomit. I was already nauseous and still had half a cup to go. We sat in companionable silence while I finished. The nausea was vastly improved and the lost were—distant.

I looked to Cipriano and saw his blue iridescence weaving around me to form a protective shield.

"Thank you," I said and at last, finished the broth.

"You need to learn how to create your own shield so that you can protect yourself."

I definitely needed to learn how to protect myself. Creating my own shield was just the start. I couldn't rely on Cipriano indefinitely, so I was eager to learn whatever was necessary to accomplish that goal.

Plus, I refused to go back to another asylum. I wouldn't go back. Not ever! I knew I wasn't crazy, but the voices made me feel so. The key was creating my own protection, reliant on no one but myself and learn all about my new world and how to survive in it.

"That way," he continued to say, "when you enter the dreaming, you won't be forced astray by the voices, the lost ones as you like to call them, when they start calling out to you. I want to start the first lesson right now, even though I know you're exhausted. It's that important," he told me.

"Why are the dreaming and the voices a worry?" I continued speaking to him with my mind, not trusting or willing to use my voice, *"because I'm Renascent?"*

"Not exactly. Though that's part of it, but not all of it," he said cryptically.

"Wait a minute! Am I..." My eyes flew to his face, as I watched and listened for his response, and asked in all seriousness, *"am I...like a zombie or something?"*

9

"Pena, I do apologize," Cipriano said, after bursting out in laughter and shocking the hell out of me, "but the horrified look upon your face was just too much and thankfully no, you're not a zombie. They're vile creatures!" He exclaimed.

I rolled my eyes at him, comfortable in doing so. There was no fear of repercussions here. I trusted him, a rare thing for me. There was a sense of familiarity and a rapport that had been established during my dungeon hell. He said he had been with me longer than just that dark time and maybe he had.

Were there really zombies out there somewhere? I shook my head no.

No way!

"Before we begin your lesson in shielding, I think a little

history is in order. Do you think you can stay awake a little while longer?"

"Yes, I'm fine. Honest. Besides, I've gone days without sleeping and your stories saved my sanity. I would love to hear more of them."

"I've been alive since the time of the Crusades," he began, reminding me of what he had already shared.

I nodded and settled deeper into the covers to listen to Cipriano weave his wonderful stories. He warned me before he started that this would not be a happy story and he was right.

"My father, Laurent, had been the leader of our clan for centuries. He was away from Scotland, guarding the nobility, when my mother, Arianna had been murdered by the neighboring druid clan. I was told he knew the moment that she had died—the loss echoing through his dragon soul and he died within moments of her."

"I'm so sorry," I said, at a loss for something more profound to say.

"Dragons mate for life," he explained, "and when their mate moves on to the other side, the one left behind usually follows immediately. It's an eternal bond that has never survived the separation of death, though there have been a few exceptions.

"When a female dragon is expecting and loses her mate this can change what we know to be a universal truth. She will survive long enough to deliver her offspring, then die shortly thereafter."

I couldn't imagine submitting to a bond such as that—not willingly. My parents would've made perfect dragons, I thought to myself. They were extremely connected to each other—almost, though not entirely, to the exclusion of everything and everyone else.

I was briefly allowed within the circle of their love, too bad I couldn't have stayed there. But in their eyes, I was defective. They couldn't see past my *oddness* to the daughter that I was and not the Snow White they wanted me to be.

"As the eldest child," Cipriano continued, "when my parents died I took my father's place as leader of the dragon clan. But that responsibility and birthright came with heavy sacrifices, including the loss of my brothers."

"What happened to your brothers?" I asked interrupting him. *"You told me that you were on a quest to find one of them."*

"I had two brothers. Jakoi, the middle brother and Aiden, the youngest. Jakoi died long ago, passing over to the other side. I mourn him every day," he said with a heavy heart, "he died protecting me," he confessed and then hurried to continue before I could ask what had happened, but the pain was evident.

"Aiden disappeared after being cursed and trapped by dark magic. I've searched for him endlessly through the centuries and refuse to rest until he's found."

The guilt and remorse he felt, along with his abject pain

over their loss, was pouring through our strange connection. He continued to shield me from the emotions associated with the voices of the lost, but his were leaking through unawares.

"But in my journey to find Aiden, I have found and collected other dragons along the way. First, I found Ian and then the two of us found Isabella. The twins came along next and now—there's you."

He was creating his own family, but I couldn't help but wonder what happened to the dragon clan back in Scotland.

"We are precious few. The Scottish clan has been viciously hunted by drampires and murdered for our essence. They love to strike when we are divided, especially when our warriors are away. They crave and covet our immortality.

"In their quest to become immortal, they've become a vampire of sorts—altering the very fabric and trajectory of their culture and consequently ours as well. We had to divide our clan and go into hiding. We hoped to divert the drampires from the mated dragons. We want to give them the chance to create more dragon offspring."

"*What do you mean, a vampire?*"

"Traditional vampires feed on the blood. Drampires feed on emotional energy and dragon essence."

"*Is there really such a thing as a traditional vampire?*" I asked. I couldn't wrap my head around either one actually.

He answered me with a quote from Shakespeare, "*There are more things in heaven and earth.*"

"Drampires have devised a way to syphon the life force

from others and feed upon that strong emotional energy that was reaped in the process. It's a temporary fix for them, but can extend their lives beyond that of a normal human being. However, if they can inflict a mortal injury on a dragon or more specifically, a Phoenix Dragon like me, then they could live indefinitely. But to do that, they'd have to steal the dragon's essence and force them to transfer their immortality."

"I don't imagine that would be an easy task. I wouldn't think any dragon would willingly give that up."

"No, they wouldn't and as long as my dragon heart beats, I will never give those leeches my power!" He said emphatically.

It was terrible that drampires had hunted dragons almost to the point of extinction, or at least for the Scotland clan. I wondered if they operated globally? Did they coordinate their efforts? Or did they prefer solo acts of murder and mayhem—robbing families of their loved ones all to prolong their finite lives?

"Those are good questions, Pena and we'll address that later," he commented.

Geez, it was like he was plucking the thoughts right out of head, just as they came to me. I shook my head and smiled. I needed to work on that.

"Once I became immortal and the sharing of my life force was born, drampires have tried to steal my essence numerous times throughout the centuries. Their attempts to kill me have grown tiresome. I moved around a lot over the past couple of centuries in my search for Aiden, so the attempts on my life have decreased. There have been none since moving to Kansas City.

"My people have always been magical," he continued, "and have been persecuted throughout history for these magical differences and abilities. My branch just happened to be dragons, but there are other types of clans out there," he explained.

"I was told I came from a mixed Scottish heritage. I was adopted from Scotland as an infant."

"I thought as much considering we are able to communicate with our minds and the fact that you hear and feel others," he said.

Foreboding settled into my already unsettled stomach and I felt weaker—if that were possible.

"Sister, pull back your aura. You're too weak right now to offer the healing of your essence."

I looked up to him startled. I didn't realize I could do that, but now that he pointed it out, I could see my aura circling him. It was if, I was trying to comfort and heal his weary heart and soul—and perhaps mine in return.

It was one of the most miraculous things I had ever seen, besides Cipriano and the others shifting from dragon to human and back again—that was pretty cool. Oh and flying on Cipriano's back—hard to beat that one!

I watched my aura, it was a blend of colors, but predominately white at the moment. Later I would learn that I'd been surrounding him in the white light of healing and protection —something I'd been doing for years without even realizing it.

Until I died, I had never seen an aura before and was thankful I had never seen Dr. Hanley or the guards' auras. I pictured them as being muddy and as black as evil—lacking the vibrancy and clarity that I saw in Cipriano's aura and in mine.

I had a lot to learn about this new world I found myself inhabiting. I didn't choose this path in life, it had chosen me, but I'd have to decide what to do with it.

If I didn't like this new existence, I could leave and never look back. I could allow the voices of the lost to carry me away.

Cipriano was right, I was too weak to offer my healing essence to him. I could feel the decrease in my energy from doing so. But, I didn't know how I engaged my aura to begin with, so I wasn't sure how to pull it back.

I decided not to overthink the process and simply thought to myself, *come home to me*, talking to it, as if it would understand exactly what I wanted. Surprisingly, my simple thought was all that was required because in the next moment my aura no longer surrounded Cipriano and had returned to me.

"Cipriano," I said, *"will you teach me how to shield myself now?"*

10

"Yes, let's get started," he told me. "What's something that you have always loved?"

There hadn't been a lot of things to love in my life, but I told him, *"I have always been drawn towards music."*

"Perfect, then we will use music to create a protective shield."

I loved the idea of using music as a shield. I had played with creating music as diversion during my dungeon hell and remembered those flickering golden notes and wondered whether they had been real.

I played music as a child, the piano specifically. Back when love was plentiful and freely given and I was the center of my parents' world and not the bane of their existence. I was their little Snow White, instead of their demon-possessed child.

"Yes, let's get started, but I don't want to play the piano," I said

resolutely.

"You don't technically have to play anything, as it's all mental. But if it would help you to visualize our lessons, then you could use the cello that Ian abandoned years ago. It's around here somewhere."

***

THAT HAD BEEN weeks ago when Cipriano started my musical lessons in protective shielding. He was right, it was more mental, but he explained how to accomplish the shielding in several different ways. I experimented with all of them until I found the one that suited me best.

One method for creating a mental shield of protection was utilizing bricks. They made for a solid wall of protection. I could layer them one on top of the other to achieve a barrier that was solid and impenetrable.

I found bricks to be mentally laborious, not to mention that I felt like I was back in my dungeon hell and suffocating in the dank darkness. Not my first choice.

I concentrated on weaving music instead. The process perfectly suited my soul. I loved hearing and visualizing the notes as I wove them together to form a musical tapestry that became my protection.

When I first picked up the bow and ran it across the cello strings, it was the most hideous sound and resembled a screeching cat. If it hurt my sensitive ears, I could only imagine what it was like for my dragon companions.

The others would fly away to keep their ears from bleeding—but not Cipriano. He patiently tolerated my fumbles as I learned my way around the cello and taught myself how to play it with proficiency.

Cipriano was a mentor, a friend and a father figure depending on what was needed. I would need all three over the months that followed.

I'd always been musically inclined, so it didn't take long for me to get the knack of making music and weaving the notes into a protective wall to hide behind. Eventually everyone stayed to listen while I played. The cello became my voice—speaking what I could not vocalize.

Inevitably, years of buried emotions surfaced and bled into every note I played.

Ian was a sensitive soul and I could feel his emotions when he let his guard down during these rare moments. I had seen him wipe his eyes on more than one occasion. Isabella would offer her mate comfort and support, by cuddling closer to him. Her love for Ian was quiet, yet fierce.

I asked Cipriano why Ian cried.

"We have all suffered great losses. This is the perfect excuse to release some of the emotions we keep buried, lest they bury us in return."

I could definitely understand that. Today I was melancholy and the cello resonated that fact perfectly—weeping when I could not.

I mastered the cello and learned to build my protective walls, but it still felt like something was missing and I told Cipriano so when we were outside walking. I needed the exercise to regain my strength, but I could spend hours outside basking in the light—something that had been a rarity for me since I had been a little girl thrown away.

Daylight, moonlight, starlight, sunrise and sunset—fractured or full bright, it didn't matter. Each one offered something uniquely beautiful to see and to feel.

"Cipriano," I asked through my mind, *"what am I? How is it that I can I hear all of you in my mind? Why can I see auras? When I drank of your dragon essence, your life force, did that change me?"*

"No. You are as you have always been, though only just now realized. When you died—the essence of who and what you are was finally unlocked. You, my dear Sister, are family in truth. You are dragon."

"WHAT!" I screeched through my mind.

I watched as Cipriano placed his fingertips to his temples, "Sister, volume if you please. Remember, our mind speak is a two-way street."

"Sorry," I replied chagrined, *"you're telling me that I'm a dragon—like you?"* I asked at a lower volume.

"A Phoenix Dragon to be specific or at least I believe so."

"But, you don't know?"

"No, I don't know for sure because we don't know who your biologic parents were."

"So you have no idea if I can shift or not?" I asked through mind speak, as my voice had yet to return. A blessing for all those involved. However, I *had* perfected my body language and the ability to roll my eyes to silent perfection.

"No, and you could die the first time you try to go through the shifting process. Which is why I haven't discussed this with you. I wanted you to build the strength of your shields first, as well as your stamina," Cipriano told me hesitantly.

"But as I build strength, Mia loses it. I know you must feel it too. She's weakening. You can't choose me over her!"

"I do sense it, just like I did with you. But I'm not choosing one over the other. Everything has its place and its time. Can you focus on her? Use your shields to block out everything but Mia's voice."

I could hear her in my mind and feel her in my bones. She was the most subdued of all the voices that were vying for my attention. The key was to focus on her as my beacon of calm within a screaming sea of pain and noise.

I was learning to build and control my own shields. Learning to pick out certain voices and emotions, mainly I searched for *Mia*—the little girl in my mind.

Mia was so very quiet, it was difficult to locate her. I had to concentrate and work hard at excluding everything and everyone. It took a lot of patience and too much precious time.

I needed to find her and quick, just like Cipriano and the

others had found me. Her essence was dying and I knew Mia was fading away.

I understood now what Cipriano must have gone through when trying to find me and why he kept yelling at me not to fade. It was painful to feel her and know that I might not find her in time.

"Well, okay then!" I decided, right then and there.

Whatever. I had lived far past the time I expected to. Dying under the wide open and forgiving sky would be the perfect way to enter the other side.

Reaching inside, I searched for that special place hidden deep within my soul. The place where the naive and unrealized power lived. It experienced periods of expansion and contraction as it developed and became actualized.

I had no idea what I was doing, but didn't care.

"No! You mustn't shift until you learn how!"

But he was too late. I was already lost and immersed within the essence of my soul.

11

One minute Cipriano wanted me to focus on finding Mia and the next minute I was shifting into my dragon-form. It was obvious I didn't know what the hell I was doing because hours later and well into the night, I was still a dragon.

I couldn't figure out how to shift back and finally gave up trying.

I had felt compelled to find Mia. She was in pain and crying for help. I needed to reach her before it was too late. I could feel her time was coming to an end. Her essence weakening—hopelessness consuming her.

I understood that feeling all too well. I'd lived in that dark place too, where all hope was lost and you just wanted to die, take your last breath and cease to exist—once and for all.

I wanted to save her from dying without hope, dying without knowing or feeling love once more. I would give her that. I couldn't erase what she was experiencing right now, but I could teach her, as Cipriano had taught me, to embrace those dark, lonely places and channel those feelings of worthlessness and shame into something positive and worthwhile.

With no consideration for the consequences, I had thrown myself recklessly into that pool of power. I had no idea what to expect or how to do it. We had never spoken about the mechanics of how Cipriano and the others were able to shift. They just seemed to do it and with little thought.

Initially it felt like I was immersed within a kaleidoscope of colors—euphorically floating on a current of peace and quiet and yet, I felt stretched and scattered all at once.

Concentrating hard, I pictured a dragon in my mind and then became one, just like that. Though I was kind of a small one.

I entered my new dragon body and saw that my world had been completely transformed. All my senses were hypersensitive and acute. It must have taken a moment for me to recover from the shift and become acclimated to my new form because I found myself gently cradled in the palm of Cipriano's hand.

I looked up at him with my new dragon eyes and thought to myself, *oh shit*, I really screwed up! I must be tiny as hell if I could fit into the palm of his hand.

"You are far too reckless little one, but you did it! You shifted into a beautiful dragon and with no help," Cipriano admonished, yet praised me, then continued on to say, "but you need to learn to do it with more control and *after*," he emphasized, "a bit of instruction. Next time you might want to choose a more proper sized dragon, instead of a little hatchling—though you are rather cute."

Come to find out, when shifting you could decide if you wanted to be big or small and since I didn't know that at the time, I ended up very small.

I opened my mind so he could hear me, "*I know. I didn't think. I just felt compelled to reach Mia. We have to find her, Cipriano.*"

What I felt from Mia was a strange dichotomy. On one hand, her soul felt so young and fragile and yet, at the same time she felt ancient. I'd been able to connect with her, tethering her soul to mine. It was risky, but how could I not. I just wouldn't tell Cipriano. I was certain that he would tell me to pull back, that I was far too weak and healing from my own hell.

Plus, I still didn't know the ins and outs of being a dragon. Whatever, I'd learn on the fly—finding her was far more important than being a skilled and proficient shifter. I didn't feel like I had the time to learn the particulars of how to shift or how to function in this new world. I would just have to learn as I went along.

"We will find her. Have faith in that, Sister."

"*Charani,*" I corrected him.

"Yes! That's perfect. It means Phoenix."

"*Thank you, it seemed fitting.*"

"I want you to concentrate, Charani. Visualize yourself, as you are normally, and not in your little dragon form," he chuckled.

He clearly enjoyed teasing me about being so little. He had carried me back into the house after I had shifted and now we were in the great room with everyone in attendance.

"What does my Phoenix Dragon look like?" I asked, dying of curiosity.

"Besides being little? You are perfectly proportioned. Your wings are an iridescent blue like ours, but your scales are pearlescent and flame red too. An unusual combination, yet we all have our differences. I'm curious to see what happens to your hair when you shift back for the first time."

"Is that why Ian and you have a section of hair that's a different color? I asked them.

"Yes," answered Ian, who had a black in his auburn hair, "and poor Cip got the short end of the old man stick with his dark hair and white stripe."

We all started laughing. I was giggling in my mind and thought of myself belly laughing in truth and the next thing I knew, I was sitting on the floor laughing out loud. I didn't even recognize my own voice, until I realized I was the only one laughing and the room was completely silent.

My husky laughter trailed off and stopped altogether, blushing.

"What a beautiful sound," Cipriano said, "I never thought

to hear you speak or laugh for that matter," he continued, his voice raw with emotion.

"I...I didn't think about it," I said, my voice sounding unusual to my ears. Husky from years of disuse.

"Sister, I truly hate to point this out to you, especially as we are all having such a wonderful moment laughing at Cip's expense," Isabella began, her sweet voice hesitant, "but when you shifted you...um...you forgot to shift yourself into..." she trailed off, clearly not wanting to say it aloud and twirled her finger in a circle in my direction.

At first I was confused, why was she pointing at me all shy like? But then I looked down at myself.

"Well, hell!"

Nope, no clothes at all. I was as naked as the day I was born. I burst out laughing because honestly it was just too funny. I didn't know how to do anything! Though I did manage to shift to my dragon-form and back for the first time and without too much trouble. And I lived to laugh about it.

I felt Ian place his jacket around my shoulders again and clear his throat. He turned away and chuckled under his breath. The twins had a sudden interest in the fireplace and Cipriano was looking down at his hands.

"I'm sure that I'm not the only one to screw up while shifting for the first time," I said.

I put my arms into the jacket and zipped it up. Luckily, since I was only about five foot seven and Ian was well over six foot, his jacket was long enough to cover all my lady bits.

"Actually, Charani, you've done remarkably well. You're a true Phoenix, just as we thought," he said as he walked over to me and placed his hands on my shoulders. "Welcome to our dragon clan—your new dragon family."

I was mute as I processed all that had occurred this evening. I shifted for the first time and lived. I was a true Phoenix and had the red section of hair to prove it. I had family now, including my Mia.

It was that concept that was the hardest to believe and to process.

Family.

I would test the strength of that bond repeatedly and what it meant to be a family, but especially a family of Phoenix Dragons.

12

I had transitioned through and survived my first shift to dragon. I felt like celebrating, but I was too tired to contemplate it. I said goodnight and walked back to my bedroom with as much dignity as I could manage—considering they had all just seen me naked. I laughed, shaking my head at myself and my little dragon hatchling.

Exhausted, yet wide awake, I snuggled under the covers, still warm from my shower and thought back over the night. I could have died again—yet didn't. Why was my life spared when others weren't?

I was nothing special and felt like a complete fraud. I had nothing to offer and could hardly help myself, let alone anyone else.

Unable to form a plausible explanation as to why, I put it aside and played with the weaving of my protective shield. Music danced through my mind and I found that it was much easier to create and maintain now that I had shifted.

I could open and close the shield at random—allowing the voices of the lost and their accompanying pain to penetrate the shimmering notes. Or, I could keep them muted and at a distance.

I would need to remain vigilant to avoid being blindsided by incapacitating pain and noise that accompanied the voices of the lost.

The missing piece had indeed been my dragon. I could feel the difference now that we were one—blended and indistinguishable.

Cipriano thought that I might be a soul seeker and attuned to the lost and dying souls of dragons and our brethren. They were normals that had the essence of our dragon running through their veins, though dilute.

My heart ached for these strangers who were dying lost and alone. Were they mute, like I had been? Crying for help and begging for mercy didn't worked. No one could hear, no one cared, and no one would come to their rescue. They were forlorn and forsaken.

I knew the feeling all too well and felt the same way until Cipriano rescued me. I was consumed by hopelessness and had accepted the inevitable—my imminent death. I had just died when Cipriano had found me. He pulled me back through the veil with his dragon essence to make me Renascent.

I still struggled with these feelings. They would sneak in and catch me unawares, sabotaging all my progress with their need to consume me.

Why was I allowed to be risen? Why did I survive that first shift? Was it so that I might rescue these others? Perhaps.

I had been hearing and feeling voices since I was a little girl. I wanted to shut them off and never hear them again, but they'd been with me for so long that the total lack of noise might be intolerable and deafening.

The individual voices had changed over the years, but they echoed the same refrain—pain, hopelessness, and despair. I could feel them, but not necessarily understand what they were trying to tell me.

Sleep finally pulled me under and my mind wandered as it contemplated the ultimate question of why?

Why had I been saved?

Why could I hear these people, but more importantly, what was I supposed to do about it, if anything?

I was drifting in the dreaming when Mia and the others found me. There'd be no rest for me tonight!

It was an odd, disorienting sensation to rise up as a shadow and not as a body of substance. Cipriano and the others had shifted to mere shadows when they rescued me from that hellhole of an asylum. I had no idea that I'd be capable of doing the same.

I decided to let the *shadow-me* go wherever it wanted— neither directing nor fighting the current I found myself drifting upon. Opening the shield that surrounded me, I let Mia and the others all the way in. I could hear one distinct voice vying for my attention, but not the one that I wanted to hear and help most of all—Mia.

She was quiet, saying absolutely nothing. It felt as if she'd given up on everything and everyone, including me.

I was failing her.

Why speak when no one would listen. I tried connecting with her, I wanted her to know that I could hear and feel her, but I couldn't tell if I was reaching her.

I hated this feeling of ineptitude, but I was a neophyte in my new world. I needed instruction and time to assimilate, but those were the very things I lacked, although Cipriano was teaching me all that he could.

As I floated along, one voice became more insistent and felt more desperate. I was pulled in the direction of his pain. Perhaps if I could release this man from whatever was tormenting him, he would release me in turn. With one less voice demanding my attention, I could focus on Mia.

I couldn't understand what *Ralph*, I decided to name him, was trying to tell me, so I followed his distinct pain signal instead. The strength of it made made focusing incredibly difficult and it resonated through me in stabbing waves of agony. If my shadow self could have wept, I might have let the tears flow. I didn't like to lose control, so I doubted it.

I arrived at an old building and hovered outside. Black

and green mold clung to the old bricks. A light mist hung in the air and coated the broken and cracked windows.

I knew I was at the correct location because dark magic surrounded the building and acted as a repellent for normals.

From what Cipriano had taught me, drampires liked to move into areas that were in desperate need of gentrification like this one. Older buildings that had been abandoned and neglected were perfect for drampires' dark magic activities.

They chose to inhabit areas that were rife with criminals. These were normals that would look the other way and mind their own illegal business. Perhaps if the cities paid more attention and took some responsibility for these areas, the criminal activities would decrease.

Drampires thrived on manipulating the minds of normals and especially criminal normals. Propaganda and rhetoric properly worded and presented in the correct light, were a powerful tool in the drampires' arsenal. And normals could be easily swayed and deterred.

There were numerous cases throughout history to support this point. Various leaders who had abused their position of power to catastrophic social results. Drampirey at work in the background to serve their own nefarious purposes—that of harnessing the physical and emotional suffering of normals and feeding off of that powerful energy.

This was a short term fix because it took dragon blood, a ceremonial knife of Damascus steel, and glyphs to have any kind of longevity. Drampires preferred dragons and their brethren, but in a pinch, mass pain would work for the emotional reaping it would provide.

I could feel Ralph inside the old building, but I could no longer hear him. I made my way through one of the broken windows. I had no way to prepare myself for what I found inside.

I floated towards Ralph and made a circle around his body. He was secured to a chair that had been bolted to the concrete floor. His arms were pulled tight behind his back.

His right shoulder was grossly deformed—dislocated or broken, I couldn't tell through the dark-purple mottling. His wrists were bound with grey duct tape, as were his mouth and ankles.

His dark head hung listlessly against his motionless, bloody chest.

He was covered in strange tattoo-like carvings—words and symbols that glowed with a greenish light and felt like pure evil.

Glyphs!

I would have shivered if I had the body to do so, but my shadow form did waver.

I shifted, remembering clothes this time. My senses were immediately assaulted by a stinging, burning sensation. I ran my hand under my nose in an attempt to relieve the feeling. Looking for the source of the irritation, I found nothing and no one, except Ralph.

Eventually, I came to associate that stinging sensation

with either fear or dark magic. It reminded me of the fear and the accompanying stinging sensation I had felt from my adoptive mother, but lower on the intensity scale.

The strength and force of his agony lingered in the warehouse—permeating the entire space. His pain moved through me in nauseating waves. It was as if he were still being tormented, but looking at Ralph, I could see he was well beyond pain and suffering.

I was too late, I thought with sadness.

There was no residual dragon essence that I could detect—only his pain remained. I wondered if I should attempt to revive him, like Cipriano had revived me. Could I offer him the sustenance of my essence—the healing of my aura if he was already dead, like I had been? How would he accept it, if he was well on his way to the other side.

Lifting my hand, I was astonished to see that it glowed with a mixture of colors that looked just like my aura. The white light of healing had blended with the blue and red iridescence of my Phoenix Dragon.

I reached out my trembling hand to touch the place on Ralph's neck where his pulse should beat and my legs collapsed under me with the force of his pain. I vomited the contents of my stomach onto the dirty floor.

My mind was instantaneously captured and assaulted.

13

Visions of Ralph's torture flashed through my mind in rapid succession and they left me in a tangled, chaotic mess—the echo of his memories felt as if they were mine and experienced in truth.

Just like that little boy when I was eight years old.

Weak from the continuous stream of memories and the residual pain, I remained on my hands and knees awaiting the next expulsion from my queasy stomach. I hated throwing up!

Once I finished weaving my musical notes, the pain started to subside and would hopefully arrest the need to vomit again.

Sitting back on my heels, I wiped the vomit from my mouth with the back of my hand and concentrated on reinforcing the mental barrier I had haphazardly created.

What in the hell was I supposed to do now?

While immersed in Ralph's memories, I'd seen a man who *had* to be a drampire. It was the only explanation that made sense. He'd been torturing Ralph and reveling in the pain he inflicted.

The drampire's features had remained distorted through the haze of pain consuming Ralph's mind—except for his eyes. They were glowing green just like the words and symbols carved into Ralph's skin.

Oh God! I did not want to touch Ralph again, but I had to if I wanted to know more about his killer. As I reached out, I noticed my hand no longer glowed with healing light. But before I could touch him, Cipriano materialized before me and prevented me from doing so.

I fell flat on to my ass—heart racing and startled spitless at his sudden appearance and booming voice, "No, Charani! You mustn't touch him," Cipriano admonished, "once was enough," he finished in a more temperate voice.

"A little warning next time...if you please!" I rasped with a show of bravado I didn't feel.

"I do apologize, but I didn't want you to be become trapped in a memory-loop tainted by dark magic," he explained.

"A what?"

"See how he's been marked with multiple dark magic glyphs?"

"Yes."

"Unfortunately, as you know, those ancient symbols and

archaic language are used as part of the reaping ritual to hijack emotional energy and acquire immortality for the drampire."

Yes, I did know. I thought about my glyph, the one that had been carved between my shoulder blades, like a tattoo—courtesy of the deceased Dr. Hanley. Luckily, mine didn't glow with dark magic, not anymore at least, despite the druid blood I wiped across it.

Cipriano continued, "When they are used in tandem, they capture and syphon painful emotions created during the torture of our brethren. That energy is funneled directly into an object infused with dark magic, like Hulbetto's Amulet of the Dead."

"Is that what happened to your brother?" I asked, sensing that it had. "*He was captured and locked into something?*" I finished with mind-speak because abject horror had closed off my airway and stolen what was left of my raspy voice.

"Yes, Hulbetto used dark magic to trap Aiden within the Sword of Dramascus."

My stomach dropped again, as the realization as to what could have happened just now. I could have been captured in a drampire trap.

"Yes, and I didn't want you to be likewise captured and cursed to such a fate. During the reaping, the drampire use a ceremonial knife made of Damascus to perform the carvings and the torture. It's toxic and incapacitating to dragons and dragon brethren. It can be paralyzing, which is why we are so vulnerable to it. Also, a small amount of blood is needed to complete the process for trapping the dragon's essence and their energies into the amulet or whatever object is being used to house the stolen essence."

"Do you think Aiden is still trapped?"

"Yes. I believe he still lives sentient and aware in the Sword of Dramascus, so named for being made of Damascus and infused with potent dark magic. I think he must be soul-tortured, as he's forced to take the life of our dragon brethren. I will not rest until I have found and freed him from the enemy!"

Cipriano's pain and angst slammed against my shield and I felt it waver under the force. No doubt I would have ended up prostrate and curled-up into a fetal position from the strength of it, but luckily I had just reinforced the shield moments before.

"Pray forgive me, Sister. But the emotional trauma that Aiden must feel as he's been forced to kill dragons and our brethren is more than I can tolerate. I must find him!"

"It seems we both have people to find. My Mia and your Aiden —my brother as well, as of right now. I will help you as best I can, Cipriano. Your quest will be mine. We will find them both and bring them home."

"Yes, we'll find them eventually. Did I ever tell you that Aiden was named after the Celtic sun god? His name means, "fiery." It fit his Phoenix Dragon and his temperament perfectly. We must take care of Ralph and his continued post-mortem torment."

I had no idea what to expect or what to do and so I followed Cipriano's lead. He shifted to his dragon form and I did so as well—and ended up as a small hatchling—again.

"Dammit! Why is it so difficult?" I said, frustrated that I couldn't get this one thing right.

"You'll get there. Be patient," he responded before instructing me to move to his side.

He opened his jaws and let loose a stream of dragon fire that engulfed poor Ralph. Horrified, yet compelled beyond reason, I did the same. But my little hatchling's dragon fire was nothing compared to his. Mine would hardly light a bonfire let alone incinerate a body—which his had done with alacrity.

"Why did you do that?" I assumed it must be for the same reason they had used their dragon fire at the asylum.

"We needed to stop the cycle of pain to prevent the drampire who had created those glyphs from using them to fuel his immortality. But, we also needed to prevent normals from finding this body—especially as it was—bound to a chair and littered with glyphs. We don't want the normals to suspect that others exist."

"Why did I feel the need to help you?"

"Because dragon fire is instinctual and despite your hatchling form, you still knew it, but more importantly you felt it."

I had so much to learn about living in this new world.

Living—what a foreign concept. I had been existing before

now and barely that. I didn't know the first thing about freedom and living unrestricted.

"Do you think you can shift back to shadow?" Cipriano asked as we turned to leave the warehouse as dragons.

I shook my dragon head and added with regret, *"I don't think so. I didn't shift into that form to begin with. It just happened when I was sleeping. Honestly, I was lucky to shift to human and then back into my hatchling form."*

"Hop up onto my back and I'll get us home and when we get there," he informed me in his fatherly voice, *"we will sit down and have a discussion about what it means to be family. Like communicating what you're doing and reaching out for assistance when you need it. There's no shame in needing help."*

I knew he was right. I should have reached out to him when my shadowed self was following that magical trail. I would next time, I told myself and apologized.

As we were flying over the warehouse and across the night sky towards Kansas City, a sensation came over me that was reminiscent of one of my more *memorable* bouts in solitary confinement.

The sensation that day had started out just as insidious, barely there and unrecognizable for what it truly was— hundreds, if not thousands of tiny black ants crawling all over my unprotected skin. I was bound and helpless in that dark hell of the asylum basement.

It was horrible!

What would the sensation turn out to be this time?

14

The creepy-crawly sensation came and went over the next few weeks, but I couldn't place what it was or from where it originated. At least not initially, but the feeling was at its strongest when I was at my most vulnerable—asleep and in the dreaming. There was something about being there that allowed me to connect easier with others—if I wanted to—and sometimes when I didn't.

My goal was to hunt down Hulbetto, locate the dragon brethren being tortured, and find Mia before it was too late. They had all become my reasons for living and the purpose to my life. I wanted to find them and free them from the hell they endured, but especially Mia.

I no longer ignored the voices, but actively sought them out and listened to what they had to tell me. Not that I understood half of what they had to say.

I kept those goals foremost in my thoughts as I discovered

what it meant to be a soul seeker. Cipriano taught me all that he could, but some of what I needed to learn would have to come through trial and lots of errors.

My dragon was still small and I couldn't always shift on command. I was hindered by the inability to reach my full potential. Something was still missing and holding back my transition to a full-fledged Phoenix Dragon.

It was frustrating, to say the least!

I learned how to take advantage of all my normal senses and all the ones that weren't—including dropping my shields to allow the voices of the lost to come in and find me. And boy did they.

Every. Single. Night.

My shadow self was compelled to respond every time—shifting to follow their pleas of mercy. The resonance of their pain became easier to track as I became more proficient and familiar with the various auras emitted and the stinging sensation of the dark magic tainting the pathway on my way to them. But despite these changes and pinpointing where my brethren were located, I was always too late.

Every. Single. Time.

The dragon souls I connected with had died before I managed to reach them.

Every. Single. One.

I was no soul seeker. I was a complete failure and should change my title to *corpse finder* instead.

Could Hulbetto know that I was coming? I was continually one step behind—often just minutes too late. I was tracking him through the dead and the dying, but maybe he was doing the same.

At times I felt as if someone were watching me, tracking me through the dreaming as I tracked the voices. Was Hulbetto using Hanley's druid blood to find me as I used it to find him?

I needed to ask Cipriano, I had kept this to myself thinking that perhaps I was just imagining things. The feeling was just vague enough to make me doubt myself and my developing abilities.

Tonight, something had dramatically changed. I'd been able to connect with his current victim immediately upon falling asleep and when I entered the dreaming. She had been right there and screaming for help. It was as if she had been specifically waiting for me.

I had stopped shutting out the voices. I learned to find the energy trail created by the pain and suffering of the brethren and follow it directly to its source.

However, this time was different, as were the circumstances.

The desperation of this woman came from the fact that she, as well as her daughter had been taken. Her pleas for mercy and for help were not for herself, but for her little girl.

The energy fueled by her love and fear were the strongest emotions I had ever felt!

Her desperation was a beacon—a magnetic force pulling

me rapidly from my bed and into my shadow self in quick succession. Something that I had yet to accomplish on my own with any rapidity, and yet here she was, practically dragging me to her. All I had to do was hold on for the ride.

This is what I imagined a mother's love would look like. What it would feel like—self-sacrificing and all encompassing.

I would save her *and* her daughter this time. I was no one's hero, but that was the only acceptable outcome. I would not let Hulbetto win again.

I had been so close to saving Ralph, but too late nonetheless, just like all the others. This losing streak needed to change, but this time I needed to save two people and not just one.

I could hear her daughter too. I could feel her pain and confusion. The feelings were a little too close to home—too reminiscent of what I had gone through as a child. Residual fear coursed through me and shook me to the core.

No child should have to experience this.

Through my connection with the two of them, I could feel and sense Hulbetto. It was like they were able to amplify him and his evil-essence. It was that amplification that would make all the difference.

I felt a positive shift, perhaps I'd win this time and save them. I quickly tethered myself to them and followed their energy trail straight into the heart of darkness.

15

Time had been essential, so I left without saying a word to Cipriano. I should have reached out with mind-speak to alert him to the fact that Hulbetto had struck again, but I didn't.

I didn't want a lecture as to how I wasn't ready to take him on. The time would never be right. If I was truly a so-called *soul seeker,* then I needed to start using that ability so that it could grow and evolve—and me with it.

The time for patience and caution had passed!

There was a thrumming sensation running through my veins, so I knew I was near. Dragon blood? Or druid? I didn't know and frankly, I didn't care. I would use whatever I had or needed to get the mission accomplished and save them.

The mother and daughter's energy signals were pounding in my chest and resonating through my soul. That's how I would ultimately find them—soul to soul. All these people that I found carried dragon blood, no matter how dilute. Dragons had been around since time immemorial.

There were lots of normals with dragon blood, more than I would have suspected. But if they had more than a trace, I was able to connect with them. What percentage that was, who knew, but they had to have a certain amount to be detectable by my weird soul-seeking ability.

I didn't recognize where I was, but I thought I might be on the outskirts of Chicago. There was a waterfront area with abandoned buildings, just like where I had found Ralph. A water element was integral to the drampires' dark magic, as was soil from their home country.

My shadow self wavered when stabbing pain hit my stomach. It was so strong I spontaneously shifted. I fell over twenty feet in human-form before I managed to shift to my dragon. My dragon had graduated to the size of a dog, so in other words, I was still small. One day I'd be full-sized, or so I hoped.

My wings caught a thermal swirling between the old dilapidated buildings and I rose with it. Traveling in either my dragon-form or shadow-form was an exhilarating ride. I loved the freedom these alternate forms afforded me.

I would rather die by my own hand, than forfeit this feeling. I would never tolerate the confinement of an asylum again, especially after tasting and knowing such freedom.

I loved the sensation of air flowing across my dragon

scales. Individually my scales weren't much to look at per se, but their coloring was unique, I'd been told. They were variegated with a blend of Phoenix-red, Dragon-blue, and a delicate pearlescent.

In addition to the beauty they presented, they collected and collated information. They sensed and perceived various stimuli and sent the perceptions to me for analysis, behaving somewhat like a computer.

I could tell by the resonance of the mother-daughter beacon and the oppressive feeling of the warehouse I approached that I was where I needed to be. The dark magic implemented by Hulbetto would deter normals from venturing too close to his building or any attempts to breach the doors to his inner sanctum.

I would not deter me!

I shifted back to shadow to be less detectable. Though I doubted I'd be able to sneak up on Hulbetto, but I was going to try. Once inside the building I followed the trail straight to them.

It felt like I had travelled back hundreds of years with the way the interior of this enormous room had been renovated. The floor was covered in soil and I would bet it had been flown in from Scotland.

Druids had a close connection with the earth, but drampires had turned their backs to these earthly ways. I was surprised Hulbetto would carry on with this tradition. There was power in the ancient soil and it was sure to be infused with dark magic. I was leery of stepping on it.

I wanted to learn all that I could about my drampire enemy and had absorbed all of what the others had told me. Cipriano and Ian had the most experience and knowledge about drampires, they had touched all of our lives.

My glyph was connected to drampires via Hanley's druid blood and I hoped it would help me to save more dragon brethren. I needed every advantage I could find to defeat them, especially the older, more powerful ones like Hulbetto.

Where was he hiding?

At the center of an immense room was a large rock that looked like a flat cairn, again from Scotland. It reminded me of the standing stones in England—though on a much smaller scale. The rock was discolored and deeply stained with the blood of my ancestors, a testament to the atrocities my dragon brethren had suffered.

I could feel the echo of the pain and suffering—both ancient and current—as mother and daughter lay immobilized on the rock. I could no longer feel the mother and realized that I was yet again too late. The stabbing pain that had caused me to spontaneously shift had been her killing blow.

Hulbetto wasn't there, or not that I could detect, so I floated towards the rock in the middle of the room.

The mother was littered with more glyphs than I had ever seen and she'd been brutally eviscerated. The rock bore yet another dragon death.

Her daughter had several glyphs carved into her delicate skin and each was glowing green with dark magic. She was young, younger than I had been—maybe five. It was hard to tell. She wasn't speaking and her gaze was fixed, staring up at the ceiling. I rushed to her side.

She was dead.

16

I grabbed the little girl and pulled her into my arms—dropping to my knees.

I was an utter failure as a soul seeker. Would I ever be in time?

I wanted to die with her in this moment. I wanted to escape the never-ending struggle. The constant strife and misery. I wanted to make a difference and find the souls that were suffering and deliver them from hell.

I didn't want to destroy what was left of them with my dragon fire!

My efforts were worthless. I was worthless.

Despair gripped my heart in a brutal vise. I could feel what little hope I had accumulated exsanguinate from my dying soul—bleeding one painful drop at a time. Just like the mother behind me, we had both tried and failed to protect her daughter.

Tears slid freely down my face, something I hadn't allowed in years. I wept for *all* of the lost. I wept for this little girl and all that she would miss.

I wept for her dreams—never to be realized.

I pulled her limp body tighter against my chest and screamed as loud as I could, "Why!" Not caring who heard my rare outburst.

"Why?" I sobbed softly, my eyes shut tight. Tears escaping to anoint her neck.

"I'm so sorry little one..." I whispered, my voice raspy and small, "so sorry."

With my eyes shut, I didn't see that my aura had surrounded her in the white light of healing. She was alive and I didn't realize it until I heard her weakly within my mind.

My eyes widened and I looked down at her face. Her eyes were closed, but I saw a lone tear slide out. Her curly auburn hair was wound around my arms, as if seeking life.

Gently, I placed my ear to her chest and heard her heart stuttering—just as mine had been when Cipriano found me in the dungeon.

I didn't think, I just reacted and gathered my dragon essence and prepared it for her.

"Drink, little one," I frantically implored, "drink of my essence and be Renascent!" I rasped into her ear.

Whether she understood or not, I don't know, but thankfully she accepted my offering—a necessary component. I gave her my dragon essence without reserve and I felt the shift. I was weakening, but I didn't care.

She was growing stronger and would live. That was all that mattered. I would forfeit my life for hers and happily.

I finally got it right! I saved a life, but that thought was tempered by the fact that I had lost one too.

I could see that my essence was reviving her and because I had the ability to heal as well, her injuries were disappearing. Her color improved to the healthy glow of youth.

She opened her solemn amber eyes to look up at me and the rush of maternal feelings I had for this young girl were unexpected. I would die to protect her, just as her mother had.

I arched my back as I was hit with a burning pain that sliced across my back from left to right in a ripping arc that felt like fire.

17

"I see you made it in time, well..." Hulbetto said, trailing off with the unsaid implication hanging in the air between us.

He had taken me unawares. Where were all those wonderful dragon senses when I had needed them?

I shook my head. I still had a lot to learn. I projected with my mind to Cipriano exactly where I was and added an apology and to hurry.

I saw Hulbetto's glowing green eyes and smug evil face for the first time from where I curled my aching body around the little girl in my arms. I was determined to protect and shield her.

He had his hands resting on the hilt of a sword. It was resting on its point in front of him like a staff. Blood—my blood dripped from the blade to soak into the soil at his feet.

I refused to answer him or cry out in pain, even though

the pain was excruciating. Staying curled around the girl, I took slow deep breaths and pushed the pain aside—easier thought than realized.

"Pray forgive me, My Lady," a voice whispered apologetically though my mind. The words weighted heavily in grief and remorse, *"I cannot control his strikes, no matter my wishes."*

I tried to focus on the words, but it was difficult through the haze of pain.

Focus, Charani. Focus!

"Tell my brother to break the sword and destroy me! I can no longer endure the blood of our race upon my hands and staining my soul."

"Aiden?"

"Aye, My Lady. Tell him..."

He faded away and said no more. I was left with a lingering sense of desolation, but before that feeling could disappear, I snatched a remnant of it, tethering it to my soul for safe keeping—if I survived.

I only had brief glimpses of Hulbetto through the eyes of his victims, so I hadn't known what to expect. And like most things in life, the more time you had to think upon a problem, the larger it seemed.

I expected to find someone larger-than-life, not diminutive in height. However, the evil emanating from him, coupled with his muddy, yet magic-enriched aura made him seem larger.

The hate I felt for this man—this drampire—eclipsed all

other emotions in this moment, until I was consumed by it and channeled that hate to alleviate the debilitating pain. I placed the girl behind me, but away from where her mother was and turned to face Hulbetto.

I wouldn't give him the satisfaction of knowing he had scored a debilitating hit and stared straight into his soul-less eyes. I stood unflinching—no small feat—as I could feel the burning laceration pull and gap open with my movements and blood gushed out to pour over my butt.

The little girl scooted up behind me to rest against my legs and curled her arms around my calf. Hulbetto tracked her movements, a predator sizing up its next kill.

"Did you know that Hulbetto was an anagram for butt-hole?" I taunted.

His eyes narrowed on me—the little girl at my feet forgotten.

Perfect.

I jumped well away from her, knowing that he would strike again and he did. He clipped the fleshy part of my upper arm and back—a twofer—with his sword. Poor Aiden, I thought just before Hulbetto struck again, clearly pissed at my anagram reference.

I was bleeding from multiple strike points and weak from sharing my essence. My dragon would be so little compared to him, but I shifted anyway to escape his next blow. The current created by his sword lifted my hair just as I turned to dragon.

I needed to get creative. He was extremely proficient with that sword and had dark magic at his disposal, plus centuries of experience. I shouldn't have come by myself, I thought briefly as an arrow whizzed by my ear. I barrel rolled to my left to miss having my head skewered.

Not fair, he had help. I should have realized an apprentice would be lurking around somewhere in the background. Now my attention would be divided three ways.

This would be so much easier if I was a full-sized dragon, but at least I was no longer a hatchling, I thought as I rolled to avoid another arrow. I primarily focused on Hulbetto, but saw the archer start for the little girl.

Oh, hell no!

I pulled my wings in tight and flew straight at him, diverting his course away from her. I pushed at her mind to run out the door. Either she didn't hear me or she was too scared, but she didn't move an inch.

I saw her shake her head.

Stubborn. Good, I thought with pride.

I saw the apprentice gearing up to let fly another arrow, so I changed my direction. Instead of avoiding Hulbetto, I went straight for him. He saw me coming and readied his sword to strike out at me.

I had my ears attuned to the *twang* of the bowstring releasing and prayed my shift to shadow would be immediate and it was. The arrow that should have found its home between my shoulder blades, was buried in Hulbetto's right shoulder instead.

His yell of pain was music to my ears.

Dropping into human-form, I reached for Hanley's reaping knife that was secured around my leg where I kept it handy. Weakness added weight to my movements, but I moved as quick as possible to strike Hulbetto with a killing blow.

He was momentarily preoccupied with pulling the arrow out of his shoulder and that's when I struck. I grabbed at the amulet around his neck and yanked with all my dragon strength. I used that momentum to pull him into my slashing knife and ran it across his exposed throat.

Blood sprayed out and I jumped back as he dropped to the dirt floor below me.

18

I was breathing heavy with exertion. Shifting back and forth had drained more energy, but had healed the sword injuries Hulbetto had scored. I turned to see where the apprentice was and couldn't find him.

The little girl ran to me and wrapped her arms around my hips. I picked her up and walked away from Hulbetto.

The apprentice ran past me and I turned to protect the girl, but he wasn't interested in me. He hustled towards his master to offer aid I thought, but he grabbed the Sword of Dramascus instead. He looked over his left shoulder at me and then took off running with the sword cradled in his arms. He didn't even glance at his master as he left.

Damn it, I wanted that sword! I'm sorry, Aiden, I thought to myself, but I couldn't leave the little girl to pursue the apprentice. Besides, I was too weak at the moment.

I gathered the little girl into my arms and walked to the

opposite side of where Hulbetto was laying. I wanted to keep going and walk right on out the door, but I couldn't leave straightaway.

I had to destroy the amulet and release the dragons trapped within. They were the source of the voices that had haunted me since I was eight years old. My dragon brethren that had been reaped of their essence and trapped in hell.

I had a dream or perhaps a vision that showed me how to release the dragons from their continued torment. I would follow that premonition and accept whatever conclusion resulted from it.

I walked straight for the sacrificial rock near the center of the room. Wanting to protect the little girl in my arms, I stayed on the opposite end of the cairn from where her mother was still laid out. Her blood hardly visible after soaking into the dirt below the cairn.

The sacrificial rock had bore witness to the death and destruction, as well as the reaping of hundreds, upon thousands of dragons and our brethren over the centuries. Let it also bear witness to the release and renascence of the remaining dragons imprisoned within the amulet. Finally, they'd have the freedom to move on. To where, I had no idea, but they'd be free and at peace.

I felt like time was running out for Mia. She was weakening and I needed to free her now.

Mia was in the amulet too, I realized. She must have suffered tremendously through her reaping to still be there.

The energy stolen during the torture deteriorates and degrades over time, losing its potency until it stops feeding the drampire altogether. But instead of being released, the dragons essence remains trapped and in limbo.

Not anymore, I would release them all.

I sat the amulet on the cairn. The chain was still attached and puddled on either side to form a linked barrier. Something about that bothered me, so I pulled the chain from the eye of the amulet and threw it as far as I could.

I wanted nothing to prevent their release.

My hands were shaking, as I pulled out the reaping knife coated with Hulbetto's blood. Just before I proceeded to follow my vision, the little girl started walking towards her mother.

Oh, God! *"Please stay here with me, little one,"* I pushed to her mind.

"Dreah," she answered, then said, "I have to say goodbye."

With that she walked the short distance to her mother. I was panicking and conflicted. The sands of time were almost gone. I could feel it in my bones that the final grains were about to fall and I would have failed yet again.

I grabbed the amulet and walked with the little...with Dreah. What a beautiful name I thought. When I reached her side she was standing by her mother.

I looked for something—anything, to protect her from how her mother looked with her abdomen slashed wide open and blood dripping over her sides. But it wouldn't erase the image from her mind or the fact she'd witnessed the whole thing in the first place.

She had to be in shock, numb from all that had transpired, but she needed this moment for closure. I completely understood that. I needed to release the dragons from the amulet to find closure—of this chapter at least. I had a feeling that I had many more chapters to go before all would be said and done, before I would find the peace that my soul craved.

"My father is trapped in there too," she suddenly said.

"In here?" I asked holding the amulet out to her, using my voice, which I rarely if ever did.

"Yes. That bad man killed him."

She looked up at me with her solemn amber eyes and I saw a level of understanding that no child of her age should have. My heart broke for the fact she had lost both of her parents to such an evil man and to such a heinous process—all so that one person could extend his life beyond what nature had intended.

"I'm sorry, Dreah."

She nodded her head, then kissed her mother upon her white cheek. I imagined what Dreah must have felt under the press of her warm lips. The skin would be cool and lack resilience, since the life had long since been stolen from her.

So brave, this little girl, and so much more than I.

She finished with her goodbyes and grabbed my hand to walk back to the other end. She sat out of the way, though close by—instinctively knowing that I needed to start.

I sat the amulet back on the cairn, this time my hands were calm. The amulet was roughly the size of my hand and very heavy. It was made of Damascus and a huge bloodstone that was swirled with the blue of our dragon essence. As I studied the amulet, I could see that the swirls were moving.

My breath caught at the implications. When my hand hovered over the amulet, the swirls increased their movement. I opened myself up to the voices, as I ran my finger across the hard surface of the stone. I could hear every one of them and all at once.

I must free them and right now!

I pulled out the reaping knife again, still coated in Hulbetto's blood and ran the blade across my palm, adding my own blood to the mix.

I slid the knife into the amulet's stone—which turned gelatinous as soon as the reaping knife touched the surface and twisted it counterclockwise. Vibrations ran through the knife as I held it still. The voices that had been extremely loud within my mind were completely silent once I slid the knife in.

Not a sound.

The knife in my hand grew too hot to touch and I had to let go when it started to burn my palm.

One person speaking is but a whisper, but a thousand whispers all at once makes for a roar—and that's when the amulet exploded into a million shards of glass.

19

I could have never prepared for what happened next. To this day, it all seems a bit unreal. It was magical and transformational. I released the dragons from the amulet and from their tortured existence of feeding Hulbetto's immortality for centuries.

All around the room and everywhere that my eye could see was the blue iridescence of our dragon essence—hundreds, maybe even a thousand or more. Too many to count and to see. I searched for Mia, I wanted to find her and I bet she wanted to find me too. She had to here somewhere.

I looked over at Dreah, she was searching the room for her parents.

As I looked about the room searching for Mia, each of the swirling essence would transform into their human-form, like stretching and expanding into what they had been before their life had been stolen. So many eras represented by the clothes they chose to wear.

After their shift to human-form, if they were able to, they would shift to dragon. At first to full-sized dragon and then down to a more manageable size to accommodate the size of the room.

Dreah grabbed my hand and we watched in wonder as this collective flew around the immense room and frolicked like children at play—happy to be free and literally spreading their wings.

It was so beautiful to watch. The emotions felt golden and bubbly, like champagne. It was such a happy feeling that I actually laughed out loud and shocked myself. After allowing their dragons free for a bit, they shifted again and back into their basic essence—the core of who they were.

The room glowed with a thousand dragons and thrummed with the contented peace they had found at long last. The luminous collection of souls turned and focused their attention on me and shifted yet again to human-form.

I watched in stunned silence as the entire room knelt before me—right fist pressed to heart. I didn't deserve their honor and acknowledgment.

"Thank you," I told them nonetheless, "you've been with me for years. I beg for your forgiveness. For years you've needed my help, but I didn't understand."

They stood as one and moved to the side. I saw that a lone dragon remained unchanged. It had not taken advantage of the freedom to shift. It hovered near the remnants of the shattered amulet.

As I walked forward, the collective shifted back. I could feel their gratitude, acceptance and understanding. They didn't know what I had been through these past fifteen years and I wouldn't tell them—ever. They only needed to know that I was here now.

"I don't know what happens next, now that you've been released," I addressed everyone, but specifically the one before me, "but won't you take advantage of the ability to shift before you no longer have the chance?" I asked.

I stopped just before reaching her and waited to see what she would decide. She shifted and just like me, she wasn't very big. Barely a hatchling, but her beautiful coloring was very similar to mine.

She didn't fly around like I thought she would. Instead she stayed right in front of me and looked me over, as if cataloguing my every feature with her crystalline-blue eyes before she shifted into human-form. Once fully transitioned, she kept her dark head down.

Everyone was attuned to us. I could feel their curiosity, as well as a palpable tension that I didn't comprehend. On top of that, there was a sense of expectation hanging in the air, as if the collective were holding their breath.

Once she shifted I could see that she was just a little girl, but not the only child in the room to have been reaped for their dragon essence. My heart hurt for their suffering and for what had been stolen from them at such a tender age.

Like the others, she had chosen her own clothes and she wore a tea-length powder blue dress with a white satin sash, white socks and black patent Mary Jane's.

My breath caught when she looked up to me. Wet lashes framed eyes that shimmered with unshed tears. It was if I were looking into a mirror and seeing the reflection of my eight-year-old self.

I dropped to my knees before her. My heart beating rapidly in my chest. I looked her over, just as she had done me. Who was she? Why did she look so much like me? I looked around for help and possibly answers, only to see numerous expressions of empathy and understanding.

But *I* didn't understand—not at all.

"You look just like I did as a child," I said to her and then asked, "Why? Please...won't you tell me your name?" I begged her, my voice raspy and clogged with an emotion I couldn't name.

"Names have power, as you know," she told me, her voice heavy with sorrow.

"I do. My given name had been stripped of its power and so I chose another for myself—one more suitable. One that I could identify with."

"Yes, you go by Charani now—Phoenix."

I had to laugh, "Yes, though, like you little one, I'm barely larger than a hatchling," I said while shaking my head at my inability to shift to a full-sized Phoenix Dragon.

"I'm the reason you cannot shift to your potential," she quietly confessed.

"I don't understand how you could possibly be responsible for my own failings."

"Have you remembered your reaping?" she asked, making my head spin with the change in subject.

"Only recently. When Dr. Hanley took over as the administrator of the asylum, only then, did I remember," I told her, the anger evident in my voice. At least he was dead now and could no longer kill my dragon brethren.

"He attempted to reap you for your essence when you were eight, but he failed in completing the ritual."

I nodded, emotions having stolen my voice.

"You named me, Mia..."

I nodded my head. I knew this had to be Mia, but I had more questions than answers now.

"...But, my name is Sarah."

I looked at her and tried to figure out how that could be possible.

"He never finished the reaping, Charani."

"No," I whispered.

"Hanley didn't finish your reaping, but what he did complete was enough to imprison a portion of your soul within the Amulet of the Dead."

The answer I had sought the whole of my life was standing before me and waiting.

Me!

"I'm Sarah, as well as you! We can finally be as one soul again, instead of divided."

"Not if I can help it!" Hulbetto said ominously from behind me.

21

I tried to turn, surprised that he wasn't dead, but before I could, he shoved his reaping knife deep into my back. Centuries of experience with reaping and killing dragons had allowed him to expertly slip the blade between my ribs and twist it with enough force to inflict maximal damage. He yanked it out with another turn of his wrist.

I coughed as my lung collapsed and blood bubbled up and out of my mouth. I spit a mouthful on the ground at his feet and glared at him while I still had the strength to do so!

I attempted to shift hoping to repair the damage, but couldn't and that could only mean one thing—the wound was mortal and he knew it.

"Now I will finish the reaping Hanley screwed up all those years ago."

My vision started to dim and I could feel myself swaying where I'd fallen. The neck wound I'd given Hulbetto was mostly closed due to the healing properties of the soil. I hadn't thought about that.

So much knowledge to acquire and to learn, but far too late to implement.

I could feel the collective vibrating with fury, but impotent to do anything about it. Hulbetto couldn't feel them now that they were no longer contained within the amulet fueling his immortality.

Nor could he see them as they swirled around him unnoticed while he prepared to sacrifice me to his greater good! He would reap me of my essence as he carved dark magical glyphs into my flesh and tortured me unto death.

I pushed hard with my mind for Dreah to sneak out. Now! I would protect her from my imminent torture and prevent her from becoming his next sacrifice. She'd been through enough.

I looked from the corner of my eye and saw her parents were urging her to leave. She was shaking her head no— again. I loved that little girl with her massive courage and resilience.

I brought Cipriano into my mind so that he could see Dreah.

"Bring her home, Cipriano. I choose her as my family, so you must care for her in my place. Lord, I would have loved her!"

I couldn't stand to know another person would be taken from her, even though we had just met—we had bonded. Cipriano would take care of her and make her family. I knew he would stop at nothing to make it happen.

I allowed him to feel my mortal injury and I felt his pain and remorse through our connection. The burdens he carried were massive and I had just added to them because I was deeply flawed and couldn't ask for help.

I was running out of time and quickly shared Aiden's message for Cipriano. I withheld the part where Aiden was used by Hulbetto as the instrument to cause me harm—I'm sure he realized that without having to live though it.

Cipriano's shock and helplessness resonated through me and almost knocked me the rest of the way over. His mission through the centuries had been to save Aiden and it was that goal, that had pulled him through each day.

Sarah, it felt awkward to call her by my name, as if I were talking about someone else, someone separate—though technically, we were separate and would remain so.

"No, Charani, we won't. Will you take me back? Will you accept all that you are? All that you could have been? And all that you shall coalesce to be?"

Sarah was a part of me, yet not. She had a profound wisdom that I lacked. An insightfulness that came from years of being imprisoned in the Amulet of the Dead and surrounded by centuries-old dragons and their collective wisdom.

"Yes, Sarah! Come back to me. Let us be as one before I die and we must join the others."

"I will, but first will you accept the collective, as you like to call them?" She asked.

"I've already accepted them. I deeply regret it took me so long to understand what they were trying to tell me all those years."

"Then prepare, Charani to be Phoenix," she said prophetically just before the room exploded in a kaleidoscope of light and color.

22

The collective rushed towards me, as did Hulbetto. Both attempting to reach me first. Hulbetto had the weight of his body to retard his movements, but the dragons were in their essential form—fast and fluid, reaching me first.

I was levitated off the floor in a thermal of buoyant energy as I absorbed what remained of their essence—en mass.

Their energy and emotions were like an infusion and I was beyond anemic and dying. I felt renewed and my mortal injuries were healed.

The need for retribution had been the impetus for the collective's decision to enter me and become one. I would do right by them. I would find a way for justice to be served.

Sarah floated up so that we were eight-year-old face to twenty-three-year-old face. She turned to look at Hulbetto one last time and I noticed he had stopped moving—eyes transfixed to where I levitated above him.

She looked back to me, before moving forward so that my dragon essence could finally be whole and complete.

A concussive force rocked the building strong enough to throw Hulbetto backwards like a limp doll and slamming him into the blood-soaked cairn. I thought I heard a crack before I was lost in a swirling vortex of fire and ice.

Like the very first time I shifted, I was immersed within a kaleidoscope of colors. The collective, both dragon and brethren, and I blended and coalesced into one—and the dragon I was destined to be.

My Phoenix had finally been realized.

I landed on the ground next to where Hulbetto lay unmoving. The cairn had broken his back when he'd been thrown against it and no amount of magic soil would be able to fix that.

The dragons and I were now one and I could no longer feel their individuality. But I knew what needed to be done.

Vengeance was mine, so sayeth my Phoenix.

Hulbetto watched as I approached, knowing his time was up. There would be no stay of execution, especially not for him. He was still benefitting from the dark magic infused soil, as well as residual immortality stolen from my brethren. It was working to my benefit in this case.

He continued to exude evil—scowling at me from where he lay broken and dying. Without a word, I reached out with my claws and shoved them deep into Hulbetto's chest. I wrapped my talons around his beating heart and held his hateful gaze as I waited for the pain to register.

Before his sight could be taken by death, I ripped out his heart—hard and fast—and crushed it before his evil eyes!

Dropping it to the ground below me, I used my dragon fire to incinerate both him and his evil heart.

In honor of the collective, vengeance had been swiftly delivered and justice served—atonement for my soul.

A wave of gratitude and peace washed over me. I *could* still sense and feel the collective. They were still with me, just not commanding me. We were in harmony.

"Charani!" I heard Cipriano yell out.

23

Turning I saw Cipriano running towards me with Ian, Isabella, and the twins hot on his heels. I remained Phoenix, which felt massive and magnificent, I must say. I was finally whole and complete and they needed to see that.

I felt Dreah come to stand next to my side, her hand resting on my hip—petting me. I understood that need. I had wanted to pet Cipriano the first time I'd seen his dragon.

We were connected—one orphan to another, though she didn't know that yet, but she would. Eventually she would understand, but more importantly feel, that she wasn't alone.

Her grief and sadness at the loss of her parents was palpable, as was her confusion as to what would happen next. Her known world had ended this night and her fear of the unknown was wholly unacceptable.

I sent my calming essence to surround her in love and comfort. I set her mind at ease by letting her know that she would remain with me as my daughter. I let her know that I was in the process of choosing my family. I had chosen her and hoped that she would have me in return.

Our bond as family was solidified with the nod of her head and the swaying of her beautiful auburn curls. She was mine and I was hers. She raised her head to watch the others approach—resolute and unswerving in her courage to stand strong in the face of adversity.

We would face that adversity together, as I was still learning what it meant to be Phoenix. It was assured that I'd screw up—a lot—especially if my most recent track record was anything to go by. Dreah patted my hip.

I looked down at her and realized that by sharing my essence with her, we had connected on a much deeper level. She was offering me comfort in return. My heart swelled with emotion and I cleared my throat.

Dragon fire exploded out of my mouth and my dragon eyes widened in alarm. Luckily, Cipriano and the others were far enough away and out of harm's way.

We all started laughing. I laughed within my mind, so that I didn't light anyone on fire. But the others, including Dreah, laughed out loud. It *was* pretty comical.

Once we subsided, Cipriano stepped up to my Phoenix and knelt before me. He placed his right fist over his warrior heart and bowed his head. Ian and Isabella followed Cipriano and mimicked his actions, as did the twins, Tarrin and Tauric.

"Stand up," I begged them, *"Please, don't do that. I'm no one's hero."*

Thankfully, they stood up almost immediately.

I shifted effortlessly for the first time and Cipriano walked forward to pull me to him. It was so comforting to be in his arms. He was my mentor, my brethren, and my brother.

Demonstrative affection was not my thing, but he was family, as were the others. Plus, I needed to set an example for Dreah, to show her that affection was okay.

Though, I guess she and I had already started that process.

"Look at you all grown up and a full-fledged Phoenix in truth," he said after stepping back—both of his hands remained on my shoulders.

I smiled, "Well, it wasn't an easy transition, but I managed to make it to *this* side, despite Hulbetto's attempts to kill me," I told them, then added soberly, "he almost succeeded."

"I'm thankful he didn't succeed in stealing yet another one of my family members. I think I've lost more than enough," he said before stepping away.

He knelt down to be at Dreah's level and addressed her directly, "I'm Cipriano, Charani's brother. Who are you little one?" He asked her.

"I'm Dreah Xavier. And you're a Phoenix, just like Charani," she said, then continued, "I know you're not her real brother. And I'm not her real daughter, but that's okay, we can still be family."

The bald honesty of children, they didn't know deception; and I would always give her the truth, no matter how painful it was.

"Charani, as well as Ian and I are the only Phoenix Dragons left in existence," Cipriano told her just as forthright.

"Wasn't she beautiful?" Dreah asked Cipriano, her amber eyes wide in wonder.

"Exceptional, just like you, Dreah."

"I have lots to tell you. But I think we should leave here now. Hulbetto had an apprentice and he could be anywhere lurking about. He's extremely proficient with a crossbow," I added, as both a warning and an acknowledgment of his skill.

I looked over to Tarrin and Tauric, sending them a quick message with my eyes and a little head bob. They were a rare set of identical twins that could have passed for Viking madmen with their blonde hair and Nordic-blue eyes. They were my quiet, gentle giants.

"My lady," Tarrin began, addressing Dreah as he came forward. He and Tauric knelt in front of her, like warriors of old.

"Would you come with us as we prepare to leave?" he asked her.

She assessed them as only a child could, but with the knowledge and understanding of someone much older. Dreah was only about five years old, but she comprehended things as if an old soul inhabited her young body. She'd been forced to grow up by her traumatic circumstances.

Tarrin continued to hold his hand out for her, giving her the option to accept it or not. I was about to intervene when she placed her little hand in his.

"Thank you, Tarrin. I need to get my mother's ring before we go. I forgot to earlier when I said goodbye. It's been passed down through our family for centuries. I wasn't supposed to receive it until I turned eighteen..." she paused to collect herself, "I'm just thirteen years too early, but I will do my best to honor the family tradition," she told us.

"Let me go and retrieve it for you, Dreah," Tauric offered, as he stood.

"No, but thank you. I have to be the one to remove it from her finger."

The twins rose and walked with her over to her mother's brutalized body. I wished Dreah could have been spared the trauma of this night. I wanted to kill Hulbetto all over again! I should have prolonged his death when I had the chance.

I wanted to go with them, but stayed where I was knowing they would take her outside and away from what would happen next.

I kept my gaze on them and stayed connected to Dreah so I could offer help if I was needed. I continued to surround her in the comfort of my essence—much easier to do now that I was Phoenix.

She removed her mother's ring and held it tight in her fist. I could feel her sadness, but courage and determination were what filled her soul.

She closed her eyes and whispered over her hand in a language I didn't recognize. I could feel a spike in her energy. Briefly, her aura glowed in her hand, before she kissed her closed fist and the energy faded away in a wink.

She opened her hand with intent of putting the ring on and my heart ached for the fact she wouldn't be able to wear it. It would be far too big for her, but when she slipped it onto her finger, it fit perfectly.

Dreah nodded her head satisfied and with a little smile on her face. She turned to me and winked, then made her way out—Tarrin and Tauric trailing behind her queenly departure.

Lord, I loved that little girl.

I looked at Cipriano to see that he'd been watching the whole scene and asked, "What do you make of that?"

"Honestly, I have no idea, but that little one has magic."

Yes, I thought, she definitely did. I would help her to realize her potential, whatever that would be.

"Let's throw some dragon fire on what needs incinerating and go home," Cipriano directed Ian, Isabella and I.

We torched everything, essentially erasing all evidence of torture. We had to protect ourselves from the normals or others discovering us. Though torture, dismemberment, and death wouldn't seem out of the ordinary to normals. Every culture had their own serial killers and murderers.

I flew my way over to the hated cairn and hovered above. There was a residual essence of pain and suffering lingering in the air. It had to be that, as it was the only thing left untouched. Memories embedded within the stone.

No more dragon brethren would have their blood spilled across that blood soaked and stained sacrificial stone—not if I could prevent it.

I landed on it with the massive force of my dragon and the weight of my vengeance. It was obliterated to rubble under me and the echo of a thousand voices trapped within were released. A choral chant of retribution and thanks filled the warehouse and we were held spellbound.

24

———

What other lost, stolen or hidden objects contained the residual essence of our tortured and trapped brethren? I knew that Aiden was trapped in the Sword of Dramascus, but who else was out there, trapped and suffering? I would locate them all and find a way to release them!

The drampire had a new enemy in me and I would revel in letting them know.

The seven of us returned home to Kansas City and Cipriano's estate. I spent some time with Dreah getting her situated in her new room, which was close to mine.

She was completely exhausted and slept after having a snack. While she took her nap and rested for several hours, I met with Cipriano and the others in the great room. We had a lot to discuss.

I shared with them what had happened at the warehouse before they'd arrived. The retelling seemed so unbelievable and if I hadn't just lived through the experience, I wouldn't have believed the validity of the story.

When I reached the moment of my connection to Aiden, I turned to Cipriano and addressed him directly.

"He was able to break through whatever dark magic keeps him trapped in the sword to give me a message. He's still strong, Cipriano, and fighting. We will not destroy him! We will find and release him. That's the only option that's acceptable. Before he faded away, I was able to grasp a remnant of his essence and tether it to mine."

Cipriano looked away as grief swept through him.

"Cipriano, look at me," I demanded gently, "I have him…" I placed my palm over my chest for emphasis, "right here. We will trace that remnant back to him. We'll find and free him," I promised.

When I explained, as best I could, about the collective and our integration, Cipriano and the others didn't seem surprised.

"There's a prophecy, a myth, a legend," Cipriano began, "call it what you will, but it has been a part of our oral histories for centuries. It foretells the birth and death of a unique dragon."

When hope is lost in darkness and death steals that final breath, a Renascent shall be born. When the essence of a thousand dragons coalesce into one, the last true Phoenix shall rise up. The dragon brethren shall be united as one. No longer fractured and fragmented, but whole and strong.

"We believe that you, Charani, are the one. The last true Phoenix. The name you prophetically chose for yourself, *Charani,* means Phoenix, as you know. You told us tonight that your true name is Sarah, which means princess. You will be the one to bring the fractured clans back together before we are extinct and there are no more dragons to be found."

"No...No, you must be mistaken. I'm nothing and no one, Cipriano, and I'm okay with that. I don't need to be someone special. I am no prophecy come to life," I denied, shaking my head.

"You have to admit, that the words and what happened to you, seem just a little too coincidental," Ian interjected, with a shrug of his broad shoulders.

"No, actually I don't admit this," I said glaring at him and he just winked.

"We want to support and guide you, Sister. You won't be alone. We will be by your side. We may not be family by nature, but we are family by choice and that makes us stronger," Isabella said thoughtfully, as she reached out to squeeze my hand.

My head was spinning with all this information and supposition. Could it be true? Could I actually be the last true Phoenix? I told them I needed some time to think about all of this and went for a walk.

I decided to take Dreah on the walk with me so that I could share an idea with her. I'd already explained it to the family and now I wanted to get her opinion since it would affect her the most. Plus, I needed some time to think over the prophecy or whatever you wanted to call it. I couldn't wrap my head around the concept of me as the last true Phoenix.

There was no way it was true.

Dreah and I went for a walk around the grounds and sat on the ledge of a fountain featuring a magnificent copper dragon caught in mid-flight. It was old and weathered with a beautiful patina to its scales. Dreah reached down to run her right hand through the cold water and I saw the ring was still on.

"Dreah, we were wondering if you would like to have a celebration dinner tonight? To honor your parents, like an evening of remembrances?"

She sat up and looked at me mutely. Concerned I had inadvertently caused her pain, I reached out to get a feel for her emotions. They were just as mute. I reached out with my hand and placed it gently atop her wet one, her ring was under my palm.

I saw auburn hair and a smiling face, an older version of Dreah, giggling and laughing as she chased Dreah and threatened to tickle her to death. She was happy and love was apparent in her voice. A tall robust man with dark hair and eyes suddenly came into the vision and swooped them both up, twirling them in a circle of love and merriment.

"Were those your parents, Dreah?" I asked, already knowing the answer.

"Yes, before the bad man came and took us away. That is how I want to remember them, not..." she trailed off quietly.

I saw what she meant, as my hand was still covering hers and the ring was still touching me. My heart broke for the visions that flashed through my mind of her parents' torture. Visions that still plagued her.

"I will help you, Dreah. We will *all* help you to remember them as you want to and eventually those horrible memories will fade and be supplanted by all the happy ones.

"The bad ones won't go away, they never do, but there will come a time when only the good memories will come to the forefront. The bad ones will fade to the background, still there, but their hold will have diminished and thankfully so."

I was still working my way through this same process myself and told her as much, letting her know that we could help each other to be stronger.

"I like the idea of a dinner to remember my parents and helping each other too. Thank you," she said as we walked back to the house, hand in hand.

We were comforting each other and solidifying our pact to slay our demons together. I wondered what her gift was. Her ring felt ancient and there was a powerful energy emanating from it, but I couldn't grasp its nature or its source.

She was insanely mature for her age and I wished she could just be a little girl happy and carefree. We had that in common, forced to grow up by circumstances beyond our control.

I would make sure that her formative years far surpassed mine. She would know love and acceptance, no matter her gifts, no matter her power, no matter her oddity.

25

The evening was a success and just what we needed. We got to know Dreah and her parents through the stories that she shared with us and in turn, she got to know us. She fit right in to our little family, just as I had.

Family by choice and by divine intervention—or so it seemed to me. The universe at work on a plane that I could neither see nor understand. We were brought together for a reason and a purpose. The key was to figuring out what and why, though quite possibly that would be impossible to do.

Tarrin and Tauric had appointed themselves Dreah's protectors and sat on either side of her. Her courage at the warehouse had been impressive and something to behold. The twins had bonded with her in that moment. They would protect her with their lives, exactly as they should. She had fallen asleep right where she sat and was resting up against Tarrin. I smiled over at him.

We went around the room several times sharing stories or events from our lives. Cipriano told several about Scotland, the old country as he liked to call it. It was clear he missed his homeland, but loved his adoptive country too.

Ian and Isabella shared how they met, finishing each other's sentences as they told their story. They shared how they knew they were mates the moment their paths had crossed.

"I wanted nothing to do with having a mate," Isabella said laughing, when Ian pinched her, "but, you can't deny what is fated to be and mates are destined," she finished, acceptance and gratitude evident in her voice.

Only mated dragons could produce offspring, Cipriano had told me before. This was one reason why there were so few dragons now. I wondered if that would turn out to be true as I looked at Dreah and contemplated her power.

Our dragon essence ran through thousands of brethren— freely given to aid a normal attached to a particular dragon. Once given, it remains part of that normal for the rest of their lives and is passed down to their children. But as the generations and centuries progress, that initial essence becomes so diluted its virtually imperceptible.

Unfortunately, these were the children that were being terrorized and suffering at the hands of the drampires seeking immortality. So in an effort to help their ancestors, the dragons had done their offspring a disservice.

I would find a way to rectify this, even if I had to hunt

down every single drampire and decimate their clans as they have destroyed our dragon brethren.

Cipriano cleared his throat, pulling me from my brutal thoughts. I looked around the room and saw that everyone was watching Dreah.

She had a faraway look upon her face as she approached me, as if she were sleep walking. She picked up my hand and placed it over her ring once she reached me.

Looking at her sweet little face, she seemed lost in her mind. Perhaps she really was sleep walking, but I knew, as well as felt, that wasn't the case. It was something else.

Her eyes were glowing from within, like light shown through amber glass.

"Look, Phoenix," she told me in a prophetic voice much older than her age, "look and know what shall be."

And with that pronouncement an incomprehensible future was laid out before me and me alone. Potential outcomes—various avenues of discovery and ones of destruction. Nothing was written in stone, yet outcomes predicated by my decisions would ultimately affect the entire dragon race.

The visions stopped and Dreah collapsed before me. I managed to catch her and cradled her in my arms. I wiped her sweaty brow with the hem of my shirt, while Tarrin draped a knitted throw over us.

The questions started, one after another, everyone wanting to know what was going on...

"What just happened?"

"What did you see?"

"What was Dreah talking about?"

"Is she okay?"

I surrounded her in healing light, but I knew she was fine and just sleeping.

"I would say that our little Dreah has the gift or curse of foresight."

"But she's so young, too young for that kind of responsibility and knowledge!" Tarrin and Tauric exclaimed.

"I imagine she wasn't to have inherited the gift until she was older, but..."

We all knew what that signified, the torture and death of her parents. Poor child.

"What did you see?" Cipriano asked.

I took a deep breath to collect myself, there had been so much and it would affect us all.

"A lot of what I saw were potential outcomes to choices that will be made now. But one choice that stood out among all the others has to do with you, Cipriano."

His eyes widened, "Please tell me."

"You have to leave, not immediately, but soon. You need to find Aiden, it's imperative. I have an idea of where you need to search, but I cannot tell you more than that."

"No, Charani, I will not leave your side. You still have much to learn. I need to mentor you."

"I know my brother. You have time, but then you will leave and bring Aiden home to us. Bring him home to our family."

"I will do as you say. You are the Phoenix, Charani. Please accept this, for all of our sakes. For the future of the dragon clans, you must."

I nodded my head to him, "I accept all that I am and all that I will become. I am the last true Phoenix."

THE END

Thank you for picking up this first book in the Phoenix Dragon Collection! Not only did you read my book and my words, but now you're reading this note as well. I'm truly humbled.

I have wanted to write for more years than I care to admit, but in 2014 decided to finally begin this journey. Thank you for joining me as I travel the many roads of my imagination.

People talk about writing and being a writer, as a solitary endeavor, but I don't see it as such. I have all of you walking along beside me.

I hope that in some small way, my stories have touched your life and you will continue on with me.

Max Andren

ABOUT MAX ANDREN

Max Andren writes Fantasy and Urban Fantasy and her first novel, Renascent, was featured in a USA Today Bestselling anthology.

The Phoenix Dragon Collection: Renascent, Coalesce, and Everlasting are the first books on her journey and the foundation for the worlds she's creating.

She started her professional career as a Registered Nurse in a Pediatric Intensive Unit. She's now a Nurse Anesthetist.

Max lives in the Midwest with her husband, their son and daughter-in-law, and their 10 year old Shih Tzu, Meme.

Be sure to sign up for my newsletter for New Release Notifications. No Spamming. No Promotions, just an email about my upcoming releases.

www.maxandren.com
email: maxandren@maxandren.com

Thank you,
Max

Let's Connect.

www.maxandren.com
maxandren@maxandren.com

ACKNOWLEDGMENTS

I could not have finished this book without the help of my Mom. She was with me from that one sentence idea—through the development of the plot and to the very end.

Thank you, Mom, for the great plot ideas and for listening to me read the ENTIRE book out loud. Even when I couldn't read through the tears, you patiently waited and encouraged me to finish. Thank you for loving my story!

Thank you, John, Ann and Jacquie—My family by choice. Thank you, Rachel and Fleur for your patience while I labored over finishing the story, the cover design, formatting, and getting the BLURB written just right! You guys are the absolute best!

Thank you, Trina for all the wonderful treats!

Max

A Phoenix Dragon Novel 03: Everlasting

Coming Soon